LANA LYNNE

The Adventures of Bo Jack

Lana Lynne

ISBN-13: 978-1-947523-60-9

THE ADVENTURES OF BO JACK

**Dedicated to
our "Bo Jack"
and
all "Tall Tale"
Adventurers
A special dedication to my grandson, Henry:
May you enjoy every adventure.**

In Honor and Celebration of
Family

Author's Notes and Acknowledgments

The Adventures of Bo Jack is based on some of the reminiscences of childhood events from a close relative's life (*He wishes to remain anonymous). However, with his permission, I have shaped these into a fictionalized story with additions and changes.

I grew up loving his storytelling ability, so when I got the chance to sit down with him, armed with a tape recorder, I relished every minute.

After typing the transcript as a keepsake for our family, I set out on the journey of the fictional Bo Jack. Our "Bo Jack" has given his blessing to this fictional undertaking. He inspired it but has allowed me the freedom to make it a new story. I've altered, shortened, or changed names or used nicknames to give anonymity to those inspiring the characters.

The small town setting for this story is not specified, but the mention of the Ouachita River will give a hint. Later in the story, some real towns and places are utilized as settings for this fictionalized story.

In working between the inspiration from the related childhood events and the fiction, I have grown even closer to my own roots. Characters have a way of magnifying the people and things we often take for granted. My appreciation for the way things were and how they not only survived but thrived has deepened. I hope these adventures cause you to look back with your families. God has a way of taking the wandering child and leading them home. The child within all of us is never lost and the adventures never end.

—Lana Lynne

* A special word of gratitude to members of my critique group: Vickie Phelps, Linda Burklin, Amber Tinsley, and Danyce Gustafson. Thanks for your refinement, prayers, and support.

* A personal word of appreciation to my new editor: Sherri Stewart, your skill and insight are invaluable. Working with you is a joy. Thank you for the privilege and polish.

* Accolades and heartfelt thanks go to Cynthia Hickey, my publisher and cover designer, at Winged Publications. Thank you for everything.

* My deepest gratitude to my father, my sister, my husband, and other dear family members. This book would not be possible without them. Our "Bo Jack" is owed more than I can express. My heart overflows.

* Above all: Thank you, Lord.

A portion of a poem by our "Bo Jack" (Used at his request and with his permission):

"It would be so nice if my grandchildren could see,

the beautiful era that once belonged to me.

There was honesty and integrity in everyone you met,

and not a soul owned a T.V. set.

We were spared its violence—domestic and crime—

It would not have been allowed during my time.

We listened to an old radio, but only once a week;

For it used a dry-cell battery that was very, very weak.

By a kerosene lamp, we would hear the news;

Then tune in to Henry A., and hear his dad blow a fuse.

We would sleep with the windows open, and smell the night air—

The fragrance of honeysuckles drifting everywhere.

As we lay in our beds looking through the window screen at a beautiful moon,

so round and serene, we would wish and hope on every blinking star.

Each one with his own dream—I wished for a car.

Poor as we were, we knew we were loved, not just by Mama, but by God above.

God took our dad when I was only two,

*but we knew His love and grace were sufficient
and true.*

*Mama said times were hard, with little pay, to
rear seven children, in my day.*

*Yet, we faced the world with all our best,
wearing hand-me-down clothes, and*
            sometimes a new flour dress.

Chapter One

A Wood Stove, a Dog, a Plane, and a Wagon

Loud cries emanated from the warmer side of the wood stove, incubating his premature-sized body inside a small shoebox. Bo Jack didn't relish his first adventure one bit. But being the last of nine siblings, he should have expected to fight his way into this world. At least, his less than auspicious—yet more than expected—entrance proved enough to get him noticed in such a busy house. Thank goodness only his family retained any memory of the four warm walls harboring the shoebox serving as his crib. His memory remained blank for the events of his first year.

After that, the islands of memory started early and remained steadfast, anchored by one adventure after another. The flash of blue sky as his sisters pulled him through the cotton patch on an old flour sack became the first to burn bright in his mind. A vestige—more a feeling than an image—of secure exhilaration from the summit of his daddy's shoulders left him too soon, but the clear recollection of being tossed in the air by his second-to-oldest brother's less secure hands by the hearth stayed with him. The latter ended with a memorable thud, knocking the breath out of him. Thereafter, his curiosity sought satisfaction with both feet on the ground.

Bo Jack loved animals. His first dog, Precious, fascinated him, and when she had puppies, it downright mesmerized him.

"Puppies out, Mama?" he asked and snapped his gaping toddler-sized mouth shut.

A chuckle and a nod gave him all the confirmation needed.

His oldest brother grunted, crossing the yard on his way to work at the mill. He turned his head as he passed their pet. "Well, it's a good thing she can feed them for a bit. We sure can't."

Bo Jack squinted at the squirming puppies, his eyes widening. "Her got milk?" His stomach growled at the thought.

Since Daddy died during his second year, food had been scarce some days, especially if you were the youngest. The serving dish might be near to or empty when it passed by his plate.

"Bo Jack, I'll send Neva out here to watch you while I go to Auntie's," Mama said, mounting the steps of the porch.

He licked his lips as he watched the puppies nuzzle against their mongrel mother's tummy. No further thought lingered in his young brain. He stayed quiet as he rolled onto his belly and crawled toward the squirming pups. Their sweet-natured mother lifted her head as he pushed his way between two of her feeding offspring and latched onto a teat. The warm milk tasted odd but good in his mouth.

"Bo Jack. Have you lost your mind?"

His ten-year-old sister, Neva, jerked him to his feet. Precious lifted her head and nuzzled her pups away as she stood, sending him a strange look. It didn't compare to the expression on his sister's face. "Well?"

He licked the last drops of milk from his lips. "Good."

The front door opened and his mother joined them. "What's he done?"

"He was nursing that dog, Mama." The look of disgust remained on her face.

Their mother sighed. "You'd better come with me for the day. It seems your sisters aren't up to the likes of you." She gave him a wink and held up her hand to prevent the obvious protest about to spew from Neva. "What was it you and Maye told on him last week? He peed in his harmonica?"

He grinned and then ducked his head at his sister's frown. His aim had been perfect in the little French harp's holes. A tinge of regret tickled him. Why did they throw it away?

His mother took his hand and tugged him across the yard—his feet skimming the ground every other step as he tried to match Mama's rapid stride. He managed pretty well until an unfamiliar drone overhead stole his focus. The pattern of left step . . . hop . . . right step . . . hop stumbled as he peered up, his eyes widening. His mother's strong grip steadied him.

"Lands, Bo Jack, what's wrong with you? We could've both fallen flat. Quit fooling around," Mama said.

Bo Jack didn't answer. The thing making the droning sound seemed to fall from the sky in a flash of metal. That didn't scare him as much as the sight of some men getting out of that silver winged thing. Where'd they come from? His heart thudded and his legs shook.

His mother dropped his hand. "I wonder why they landed here?"

Bo Jack didn't want to know. He found his feet and high-tailed it back to the house, dashing by his sisters who stood on the porch.

"Where you going, Bo Jack? Come see the plane with us," Neva said.

Plane? He'd heard about them. Still, that weren't natural, men landing and walking around something like that. No, sir—where could he hide? He eyed the shadowed place behind the door and squeezed his small frame flat against the wall behind it.

Neva followed him. "Bo Jack, get out from behind there. We're gonna miss all the fun."

He shook his head at her and resisted when she tried to pull him from his safe place. After another moment of tug-of-war, she let go and ran out on the porch and down the steps. He could hear her yelling for Mama. Tears coursed down his cheeks and his mouth longed for water, but he didn't move.

His breaths became easier when no one came. Curiosity danced right below the ball of fear burning in his belly. Still, he had no impulse to venture from his hiding place. Neva and Maye could tell him about the plane.

After what seemed like hours, footsteps sounded on the porch steps. He held fast to the doorknob but let go at the sound of his Mama's voice. The hinges creaked as she pulled away his door shield. He swallowed hard at her frown.

"Do I need to get your brother to talk to you?"

His heart quaked.

"No, ma'am."

She reached out to wipe his tear-stained face and sighed. "You have worked yourself into a fever. Come on out from there. I'm putting you to bed."

The sheets felt cool. She tucked him in and smoothed his sandy bangs away from his fevered brow, chuckles punctuating her smiles. "That was only an airplane. You should have stayed out there. Your cousin came and talked to the pilot. Now he wants to be one."

Bo Jack didn't know what she meant, but he hoped Nuben would change his mind. He didn't want any more airplanes coming by their house.

No, he'd stick to his red wagon. He could pull it and stay on the ground. Besides, it held anything he could find on his treks across the pasture, in the woods, or along the railroad tracks. Rocks, pieces of wood with favored lizards, turtles, or other things of interest made up his cargo and passengers. On special occasions, his sisters pulled him, and he trusted them with his prized possession until one dark day.

While his sisters got ready for school, he wandered outside to get his wagon. Unease and confusion filled him at the sight of the vacant place under the tree. He ran to the shed—nothing there. Panic seized him. He ran for the house.

His sisters emerged from the house. Neva ran down the steps toward him. "What's the matter?"

He gasped for breath. "They stole it."

"Stole what?" Maye asked, joining them.

"My wagon." Why did they look so calm? Frustration filled him.

"It ain't stolen," Neva said. "We threw it away."

His panic crested into anger. "No." He turned toward the porch. "Mama."

Maye put her hands on his shoulders and squatted in front of him. "It's worn out, Bo Jack. Mama said it's not safe for you. Maybe Santa will bring you a new one for Christmas."

"Where?" He couldn't understand it. Christmas was in less than a month. How could Santa fill a new wagon order at such short notice? Besides, the man in red never left much for them.

"Bo Jack, it's gone. Now, you go back to the house. We got to get to school. Besides, Aggy is coming by today."

"Really?"

Their eldest sister had married and left home before they'd moved close to his aunt after their father died. His brother, Jake, had left home too. Life kept them busy and visits scarce.

He glanced back to the empty place beneath the tree once more as his sisters headed for the road. Maybe Mama could help him write to Santa before Aggy arrived. He ran for the house.

Sure enough—Christmas came around and a wagon bearing a strange resemblance to his old one, but with much brighter paint, appeared under the Christmas tree. If his cousin from Detroit had not cut notches in his tires for mud-grips during a day visit the next summer, he'd have kept it forever.

Chapter Two

The Storm Cellar and Wash Day

Nothing terrified Mama more than a storm. The familiar pattern of left step . . . hop . . . right step . . . hop . . . stumble took over Bo Jack's feet as he struggled to keep up with her rapid pace across the field to his aunt's storm cellar.

The first time he could recollect her waking him at the height of a storm, his heart hammered against his ribs in a mixture of fear and the thrill of adventure. He'd been many times before, but this time his five-year-old brain took in everything.

The wooden doors covering the deep and damp cellar looked huge. Mama struggled to open them in the downpour. A shadowy figure beside his uncle's smokehouse caught his eye right before Mama pulled him into the depths of the dark cavern. Mama secured the doors and fumbled around in the darkness. The spark of a match grew into a bright flame once touched to the wick of the lantern. He shook the water out of his hair and wiped his eyes. In the glow of the oil lantern, his mother led him to an old wood box.

"Sit down. We'll be here for a bit," she said, removing a folded quilt from the top of the box.

He peered around and grinned. Mama pulled off his wet coat and wrapped the quilt around him. His sisters had missed out on this fun. Just wait until he got home. Then he frowned.

"Where Neva, Mama?"

"Don't you worry none. Those girls wanted to stay with your brother. Clive will watch after 'em. They are—" The deafening roar of rain and wind on the doors, closely followed by a boom of thunder, drowned out her last words. She sat on the box and pulled him onto her lap.

"Where's Auntie?"

"I've told you before. They don't mind the storms none."

Bo Jack twisted to peer up at her face. "But this is their cellar."

The fear left Mama's face and she laughed, hugging him. Part of him wanted to be mad, but when she laughed, he did too. She pushed him away to arm's length and gazed down at him with tenderness in her smile, her dimple flashing. "You're a quick one. No, you're right. It is theirs. They have it for more than storms. Look around."

The lantern's light glinted off of jars of preserves and the other results of his aunt's days of canning. Still—

"Oh, but—"

"They will come down here if a twister comes."

"Was Daddy afraid of storms?"

Her smile faded and she turned her head away.

"Mama?"

She wiped a hand across her cheek and glanced down at him with a smile. "No, son. Your daddy wasn't afraid, and he made me feel safe."

Bo Jack took her hand. He didn't like her to cry.

"You make me feel safe, Mama." The light of the lantern's smoky flickers pulled his gaze and he smiled, remembering his cousin's book from the library. "Besides, don't you see those knights guarding us? Their shadows are on the wall between the light and the dark."

Mama's mouth parted as she gazed at the wall before looking down at him. She nodded. "I sure do. We must be safe. Who are they fighting? You tell me what you see."

His shadowy visions of battles and conquests played out, distracting them from the storm. But after he narrated the defeat of the knight's foes, tedium and the warmth of his mother's lap overcame him. He slept.

Mama woke him later—he wasn't sure of time—and threw open the doors above them. The smell of a rain-fresh morning greeted them.

Bo Jack's sleep-clouded eyes missed many of the broken limbs and fence wire when they emerged. But the pre-dawn sky told him they'd spent the whole night in the cellar this time. Mama half-carried and then tugged him the rest of the way home.

Maye and Neva came out the back door with their arms full of laundry. They headed toward the heating wash pot on the fire his brother tended in the yard.

"How'd you get that wet wood to light, son?" Mama asked his eldest brother.

Clive kept his gaze fixed on the flames. "I knew a storm was brewing yesterday, so I gathered some and piled it inside, then put the pots out here to fill in the rain—no sense pumping more than I have to. Wash day is here, storm or not—right, Mama?"

Mama laughed. "It sure is. It's Monday. Thank you. Now, you girls hold up until he tells you it's ready." His sisters rolled their eyes.

Mary, his soft-spoken teenaged sister, had breakfast waiting for them in the kitchen. His stomach growled. She took his hand.

"Let's get you dressed and then you can eat. Mama, there's a little coffee on the stove for you. I'll get the quilts out on the line after I tend to Bo Jack."

His tongue went to wagging as he changed clothes. "You missed it, Mary. We went down in that hole with the doors."

Mary shuddered and sighed but smiled at him. "I'm glad you had fun, but we don't have to do that anymore. The rest of us are big enough to stay right here."

"Why?"

She shook her head, gathering up his damp things and taking him by the hand. "You get to decide what you're afraid of when you're older. We don't mind the storms now. Mama still does. Come on and help me with the quilts."

"I wanna stir," he said.

Mary pulled him back to the kitchen. She released his hand and shifted the bundle of his wet clothes to her hip.

"Grab a biscuit and that last slice of bacon off the table. You can eat them outside."

Bo Jack palmed his breakfast, munching as he followed her out back and over to the wire clothesline. She shook the quilts out and draped them over the wire.

"Ow."

They turned as Neva jerked her hand away from the scrub board and lifted the knuckles of her right hand to her lips.

"Don't you go trying to get out of helping me," Maye said, grabbing the bar of lye soap and positioning another shirt on the board.

"I'm bleeding," Neva said, thrusting her hand toward her sister.

Mary shook her head and glanced down at Bo Jack. He stuffed the last bit of biscuit into his mouth and handed her a clothespin.

"Don't you ever be that petty," she said.

"Purty?" He made a face.

She giggled and squatted in front of him. "No, petty. Acting selfish and complaining over little things."

He still didn't get what she meant, but he nodded anyway. The fussing behind him got louder.

"You two, stop that right now," Clive said. "I've got to get to work and Mama needs your help. Let that boy use the punching stick on the clothes. He's got to help some way."

"Yes, sir," Maye said.

Neva didn't say anymore until they moved the clothes from the first rinse tub into the bluing water.

"Bo Jack, it's your turn. Grab that stick."

Maye stood behind him and helped him put it in the large metal rinse tub. He punched the clothes to submerge them in the liquid. The blue tinged rinse water thrilled him. It seemed magic the way it brightened their clothes, especially the whites, but that wasn't the best part.

"Can I bathe in it first?" he asked.

"Of course not, silly. You go last," Neva said.

He frowned and let go of the stick. Maye came over to him. "Honey, you need to punch them a bit longer."

Maye didn't seem too dirty. He sniffed her as she helped him grab the stick again. She laughed in her kind way. "What are you doing?"

He gave her a sideways grin and grabbed the stick but frowned at Neva, who removed more items from the first rinse tub.

"Maye don't stink, but you might. Don't leave your stink in the tub."

Neva dropped the shirt she held into the water and dashed toward him. Mary hurried in between them.

"We don't have time for this foolishness. Besides, Bo Jack, it's too cold to bathe out here today. You have to wait 'til summertime for that. The girls aren't going to school today because of all the work that needs doing. We'll heat some water in the kitchen tonight. Clive got up earlier and pumped enough water to top off the pots for the washing and left some for baths to be heated in the kitchen."

"Clive must be real dirty," he said, tilting his head.

Mary crossed her arms and smiled down at him. She lifted her eyebrow, waiting for him to explain.

"He never bathes here."

"Does he smell bad to you? Does he have the itch?"

Hm, that vexed him a bit. He shook his head.

She let out a soft laugh, and his cheeks grew warm when his other sisters joined her. He pushed the punching stick away and took a step toward the house, but Mary grabbed the back of his shirt and pulled him in front of her. "You stay put. No pouting today—" She smoothed his shirt and squatted down in front of him. "He uses the bathhouse at the mill after work. That way your water isn't even colder by the time it's your turn. You should thank him."

His mind churned. He'd bet Clive always had hot water at the mill.

"Could I go with him? Boys bathe there and girls here?"

She didn't laugh but scanned him from head to toe. He didn't care for her speculating. "Are you big enough to work at the mill?"

He stuck out his chest. "I'm five."

"It's true—and a very tall boy you are—but not yet tall enough to run the saws. So no, they wouldn't let you bathe unless you work there."

"Shucks."

She tousled his hair and retrieved her basket.

He grabbed the punching stick but stopped, remembering a flicker from the previous night. "Hey, Mary. Someone was near the smokehouse last night, I think."

"Ah, maybe Uncle Ernst was checking things. I'll ask." She frowned. "But it could have been one of them hobos. A few hams have gone missing. Did Mama see him?"

"I don't think so."

She smiled. "You didn't ask her? I bet your eyes were just playing tricks on you in the storm. Now, no more jawing. Get busy."

He grinned and helped Maye lift out each garment. They wrung out the excess water from each piece and placed them in the basket. Mary then hung each item on the clothesline. Mama came home from helping his aunt mid-morning and joined them. They finished close to lunch.

His Uncle Ernst and cousins came by to get him. "Cora, we'll take that boy off your hands for the afternoon. I fixed my plow this morning and need to get him ready to be our water boy during planting. Spring's right around the corner." His uncle turned to him. "Come on. Go get your coat."

Bo Jack liked playing with Jimbo because he was only a few years older than him, but Nuben's teenage mischief confused him. Sometimes they could trust him but only sometimes.

Oh, boy. He dashed headlong into Maye who'd retrieved his jacket for him.

"Oof, Bo Jack. Slow down," she gasped but then laughed as she helped him shrug into the tattered garment.

Bo Jack shifted from foot to foot, wishing she'd hurry. She laughed harder, trying to straighten his collar.

"Looks like he's ready for time with the menfolk. Quit fussing over him, Maye," Uncle Ernst said. He moved to the door. "Let's go, boys."

Jimbo dashed past him, and Bo Jack ran to reach the wagon before him. His uncle still used a wagon for farming. He had a cotton field close to the home and leased a field about three miles behind their property to grow corn and oats. In the summer, the crops grew thick, and the smell of hay and dirt filled the air. Bo Jack could hardly wait until he could ride on top of the hay bales like Nuben. But for today, he'd take being asked to go.

His brothers had told him their daddy took them with him from the time they could walk. Of course, that had been at their old farm. Two other siblings had died as babies there. They'd moved from the farm where their daddy grew up before Bo Jack's birth to the house where he'd been born.

Although a dim memory, he kind of remembered the barn his daddy had built across from that house and the fruit trees. They had to sell the farm and move here after Daddy died. He guessed he missed him. Sometimes the same ache he felt about Jake and Aggy leaving home filled him when his other siblings talked about Daddy. That very feeling gnawed at his gut right before he scrambled into the back of the wagon with his cousin.

"You'd better hang on. Daddy gets the mule to clopping good," Jimbo said, grinning.

Bo Jack glanced back at Uncle Ernst and Nuben, who settled on the wagon seat. He gripped the side of the wagon and grinned back at his cousin. No, he didn't know much about what he didn't have, but he knew what he did.

Chapter Three

Hay, Hams, Hobos, and Preachers

Summer came in all its scorching intensity. Bo Jack strained his almost six-year-old muscles to carry bucket after bucket of water to the men in his uncle's hayfield. Slosh . . . bump . . . rest . . .

"Bo Jack, get your hind end over here," his cousin Jimbo called, wiping the dripping sweat from his forehead and eyes. Jimbo had been promoted from training him as water boy during planting to one of the scoopers of the hay.

Bo Jack hurried to his cousin and unhooked the tin cup from the bucket handle. Jimbo grabbed it, his hands shaking as he dipped the cup and guzzled the cool liquid.

"You okay? Your face is mighty red," Bo Jack said.

Before his cousin could answer, Uncle Ernst hurried over to them. He pressed his lips together as he waited for Jimbo to finish with the cup. "Jimbo, you go sit by that tree for a bit to cool off and then run back to the house to tell your mama we're about to break for lunch. You can ride back with her when she brings the sandwiches to us."

For once, his cousin didn't protest. Uncle Ernst turned back to Bo Jack and dipped the cup. He took a drink and then wiped his mouth with the back of his hand. "You go on and take the men one more water break. They'll be ready for lunch when your aunt gets here."

"Yes, sir," Bo Jack said, glancing back toward his cousin one more time before hurrying along.

The familiar sound of a train whistle filled the air. The field lay near enough for the piercing noise to turn their heads for a moment but far enough away not to feel the reverberations from the tracks. Bo Jack scanned the area of the familiar smokestack billows as he set down his bucket by Nuben. He frowned. An unfamiliar man ambled up the road toward the field.

"Blamed hobo," Nuben said. "I'd better watch the smokehouse tonight."

"You really think he's the one stealing the hams?" Bo Jack squinted up at him. "Clive says it could be those d—"

"Hush up with that, Bo Jack. I'm betting on the hobos."

Nuben handed him the cup and Bo Jack hooked it to the handle before moving toward the other workers. He'd given all but one man a drink when his aunt turned up in the wagon with Jimbo riding beside her. He sure recovered fast. Jimbo stuck his tongue out at him and jumped to the ground.

His aunt raised an eyebrow and motioned him up with a wave of her hand. "Bo Jack, let me look at you," she said after he complied. She peered at him and wiped his face with the edge of her apron. "You're doing fine. Are you ready to eat a bite?"

"No, ma'am. I got one more man to water."

She chuckled. "You make 'em sound like plants. Well, get on with it. I'll leave your lunch pail by the tree over there."

"Yes, ma'am."

He scrambled down and sloshed a few more times before he reached the waiting man. His rumbling stomach willed the talkative man to be quick. Bo Jack smiled when the worker handed the cup back to him. He hooked it to the handle of the almost empty bucket and hurried back for his lunch.

As he neared the tree, he found a man reaching down for his pail.

"Hey, Mister, that's my lunch."

The man straightened, holding the pail, and turned. His battered hat and tattered clothes identified him more than his grime-covered face—a hobo.

The image of the figure by his uncle's smokehouse in the storm the past spring came to mind. "Did you steal my uncle's hams?"

Confusion—or maybe a start of guilt—flashed on the hobo's face. "What?"

"I saw someone in the storm. You were stealing my pail."

"No, boy. I didn't see no one by it and thought it was a leftover," the man said, holding out the pail to him.

Bo Jack took it. Suspicion mixed with a tad of something sad churned in his stomach. He remembered something Maye had told him about their father.

"My daddy always offered a ham," he said.

The hobo frowned and scratched the back of his neck. His eyes darted from the pail to Bo Jack's gaze. "I'm not following, boy."

"If'n someone hungry came down the road, Daddy'd offer a ham from our smokehouse."

"I thought you said it was your uncle's smokehouse."

"The one round here is my uncle's. We don't have one . . . or my daddy anymore," Bo Jack said.

The raggedy man looked down and cleared his throat. When he glanced up, his eyes watered a mite. Why? "I'm sorry, boy. My daddy died in the Great War, close to the end in 1918."

"Mine just got sick," Bo Jack said. "Sorry 'bout yours. Anyway, mine taught us to offer. Guess I should." Bo Jack's stomach gave a loud grumble. "You think I might just offer you half my grub?"

The man chuckled and nodded. "That's mighty kind of ya. My name's Pete Rooney."

"I'm Bo Jack." He swallowed hard, really wanting all of his lunch. Still . . . He sat down with his pail, pulling out the slice of bread and hard-boiled egg inside.

Mr. Rooney sat down on the ground in front of him.

After making a jagged tear of the bread, Bo Jack gave the slightly bigger half to Mr. Rooney and then frowned as he studied the egg.

"You can just eat the egg. This bread will be fine," the man said.

Relief flooded him until he caught sight of the hole in the man's shoe. "No, sir. I offered half." He took two bites of the egg and swallowed before holding out the half left.

Mr. Rooney took it and popped it in his mouth. "Thank you, son."

Footsteps shuffled through the field behind Bo Jack. He turned to see Uncle Ernst approaching them. "Bo Jack, finish and go refill that water bucket at the creek," Uncle Ernst said.

"Yes, sir," Bo Jack said. He stuffed the half of bread slice in his pocket and stood, then studied his uncle's face. "Uncle Ernst, I offered half of my lunch."

"I'm sure you did. Now, go on and do what I told you."

"Yes, sir."

Mr. Rooney gave him a grateful smile and waved.

"Bye, Mr. Rooney. You gonna be around?"

The hobo's eyes shifted to his uncle and then back to him. He shook his head. "No, I'm leaving tonight. Thanks for sharing with me."

Bo Jack grinned and turned. He glanced up at the sky. Maybe Daddy could see him.

****

The next Saturday, he felt more like the hobo than the son in his family. His ever-rumbling stomach echoed hunger.

The smell of fried chicken filled the house all morning. His mouth watered when Mama began cooking after breakfast. The delicious smell drifted through the kitchen window as he did his chores. Instead of running to play by the swimming hole with his friends, he climbed the trees close to the house. They didn't get fried chicken often. He should have known Mama had invited a guest.

When the itinerant preacher drove into the yard, Bo Jack watched from his tree-branch perch near the house. His mama had fed visiting preachers before, but this one— Bo Jack swallowed when the man tipped the car to one side, unfolding his girth from the seat. Neva and Maye ran down the steps, greeting the preacher, while Mary stood in the doorway.

"Welcome, Pastor," Mary said.

The stairs creaked at the man's every step. He removed his hat.

"Lunch is ready, Pastor. Please come on in," Mama said.

"Thank you for asking me, Mrs. Talbot."

The trio disappeared into the house.

"Bo Jack. Where are you hiding?" Neva called.

Bo Jack sighed, scrambled down, and ran over to Maye.

"You'd better wash up before you go in there," she said.

He wrinkled his nose at her. "You think we're going to have enough? Is Clive coming?"

Maye shook her head, but Neva answered. "No, he's in town. He don't like preachers too much. So we got plenty."

Bo Jack liked her confidence, still— "How many chickens did Mama cook?" he asked.

"Stop it, Bo Jack. Grownups eat first, and we'll eat what's left. I'm sure it'll be fine," Maye said, taking his hand. "Let's go. Mama wants us there when he blesses the food."

Once around the table, everyone bowed their heads, but Bo Jack didn't shut his eyes long. The platter of fried chicken needed watching. He knew better than to ask for anything on his plate until the preacher had had his fill.

His eyes widened and his heart fell as the pile of chicken dwindled. Mary and Mama each took a small thigh piece after the preacher took a breast and three legs. Mama shook her head at him, Neva, and Maye. They sat quietly and watched. Bo Jack's eyes widened as the top of the chicken leg entered the man's mouth on one side and came out the other with nothing but bone left.

Bo Jack didn't even listen to the conversation across the table. The man had a powerful voice, but Bo Jack would wait until church to listen to him talk. Right now, he just wanted him to stop eating Mama's chicken.

After another round with the platter, three pieces remained. The preacher reared back in his chair. "I don't know when I've had a better meal." He smiled at Mama.

"I'm so glad you enjoyed it. We are looking forward to your sermon tomorrow. Would you like anymore?"

"No, no, I'm full."

Mama gave him a gracious smile and then nodded at Neva. She passed the platter to his sister.

Neva took one piece and Maye took one, but just as he put his hand on the edge of the platter—

"If you don't mind, I think I could eat that last chicken leg," the pastor said.

Bo Jack's heart fell into his empty stomach and tears filled his eyes. He couldn't even look at Mama. The girls wouldn't make a scene by sharing theirs with him in front of the pastor. It might make him feel bad, but when Mama passed the last of the mashed potatoes and few field peas at the bottom of the bowls, they each took small spoonfuls so he could have the rest.

Once excused from the table, Bo Jack dashed outside, tears streaming down his face and ran straight into his aunt.

"Bo Jack, look where you're going."

He peered up and the stern expression on her face changed. He swiped his wet cheeks. She gathered him close for a moment. The tears came faster, and he sobbed. Her love comforted his heart but couldn't fill his still-hungry stomach. She set him away from her.

"Dry it up, now. You'll make yourself sick. Company is here and you have time to go play. I'll help your sisters with the dishes."

Bo Jack thought about running to Kenneth's house but decided to go down by the creek and watch the tadpoles instead. He fell asleep in the shade of the trees covering the bank. Once he woke up, the ache in this stomach had dissipated. He skipped a few rocks and headed home. His sisters sat on the porch steps. Maye wiped sweat from her forehead and Neva fanned her face.

"Where've you been?" Neva asked.

"The creek."

"Wish we could've gone."

"Preacher just left," Maye said. "He really is nice, Bo Jack. I don't think he thought about you missing out on the chicken."

Bo Jack sat down on the bottom step below them and kicked at a rock. His sister's words caused him to ponder a bit. "Maye, sometimes I think hobos are better than preachers."

"You can't say that," Neva said. "I'm telling Mama."

"Wait, Neva. What do you mean, Bo Jack?" Maye said.

"Well, Mr. Rooney, the hobo I met, didn't mind me offering half to him because he knew I was hungry. He considered me. The preacher didn't."

Maye reached down and ruffled his hair. He turned and made a face at her. "Or maybe, the preacher considered you more in a way. You had to give up something you'd focused on all day."

Bo Jack shook his head, *Girls say the strangest things.* "That's good?" he asked

"It can be. Let's see. What did you learn?"

"If someone's hungry, I want to share."

"Don't you see?" Maye said. "That's what Mama did. Aunt Do fussed at her today about feeding the preacher when she can barely feed us. Mama said the community was happy to have a preacher visit, but others wouldn't feed him. Sometimes they don't even have enough of a collection for him to have money to travel to the next town, much less food. Ever since the Depression, people are careful. Mama said it's only right to feed him."

Chapter Four

Marbles and Hammers

"They ain't up here," Neva declared. "Let's go back to the barn."

Bo Jack grinned at Jimbo after the girls left the hot attic. He ducked back to the dark corner, retrieving the bowl of hidden marbles.

"You distract 'em when I get there, and I'll hide these marbles easy for them. I'm ready for a turn," Bo Jack said.

Jimbo nodded and scrambled down the attic stairs.

Bo Jack followed but detoured, running around the side of the barn and squeezing under a loose board in the back. He could see his sisters starting up the loft ladder, so he opted for the hay bales to the right and tucked the bowl between two.

Jimbo whistled and Bo Jack waved at him.

"I heard that," Neva called from the loft.

Bo Jack leaned against the ladder, Neva's foot nudging his shoulder on her way down it.

"Move, Bo Jack."

He laughed and ran over to Jimbo.

Maye smiled at him and shook her head before chasing after her sister. The girls ran from one corner of the barn to the next, looking under hay bales, shovels, sacks, harnesses, and any random items claiming the space. Bo Jack snickered until they neared the two bales concealing the marbles.

Maye leaned over and reached in, but Neva jostled her aside and retrieved them first. "Found them." She lifted the bowl in triumph.

"Now it's our turn to hide them," Maye said. "Hide your eyes."

Neva tucked the bowl against her side with one hand covering the marbles, preventing them from tumbling from the bowl.

Bo Jack nudged Jimbo with his elbow and they walked to the barn door. They raised their forearms, placing their foreheads against them as they leaned against the splintered surface and shut their eyes.

The sound of scurrying footsteps, bumps, clangs, and ill-concealed giggles filled the next few minutes. Bo Jack's breaths amplified in his own ears and his cousin's sweaty smell wrinkled his nose. "Is it bath day?"

Jimbo shifted, jostling him. Bo Jack lifted his forehead and turned to find his cousin scowling at him. "You know it ain't. Besides, you stink too," Jimbo whispered.

"Want to go swimming later?"

"Maybe."

"We can go to the Blue Hole," Bo Jack said, the thought of the cool water almost stopping the sweat dripping from his hair.

"Charlie's s'pose to come over to go fishing. We'll—"

"Ready," Neva announced from behind them.

"Did you peek?" Maye asked.

"No, we did not."

Unlike the girls, he and Jimbo split up when they searched for the marbles. Jimbo looked in the obvious places, but Bo Jack liked to hunt in the not-so-obvious ones. He could tell who had hidden them. If in one of the more expected places, Neva had hidden them. Otherwise, Maye had done it. Their minds often worked alike on solving things.

They searched for ten minutes without luck. Bo Jack knew it had to be Maye who'd hidden them. He went high to the loft again without luck, but something caught his eye as he started down the ladder. Someone needed to be on eye level with the floor of the loft to see it. He grinned. A burlap sack lay underneath a hay bale with only a fourth of the sack exposed, the top fourth to be exact, and the opening faced in the direction of the ladder. Maye—it must have been her— had slid the small bowl inside, leaving only a tiny part visible. She covered it with loose hay, but the glint of the blue bowl peeked through.

He glanced down at the bottom of the ladder where his sisters stood, stuck his tongue out at them, and scrambled back up to the loft.

"Found it." Jimbo whooped when Bo Jack jumped off the ladder with the game treasure.

"I knew I should have picked the spot," Neva said.

LANA LYNNE

Bo Jack caught Maye's eye and grinned. "No, it was a great spot."

She smiled.

Jimbo rubbed his hands together. "Last time, girls. Hide your eyes."

Bo Jack put his finger to his lips and pointed toward the house. Jimbo nodded and made noise, moving things while Bo Jack slipped out via the loose board. He'd put the marbles back in the same spot in the attic as last time. They'd never found the bowl then and wouldn't now. Once he finished, he ran back to the barn and joined Jimbo in the production of mock hiding for a few more minutes.

"Hurry up," Neva said with her face against the door leading to the corn crib.

"Done," Jimbo said.

The girls dashed into action.

After a few minutes, Jimbo stopped them.

"Wait, wait, wait," he said, winking at Bo Jack. "I forgot to tell you. Bo Jack hid them in the attic."

Neva shoved Jimbo when they passed by. He laughed.

Charlie, his cousin's friend from down the road, entered the barn after the girls exited.

Doggonit, no swimming hole today. Jimbo treated him the same unless someone his own age came over, and then Bo Jack became the little nuisance. Nope, not today. He'd find something else to play.

Just then his older cousin and his brother entered the barn. Nuben and Clive carried in more corn. "We've got to shuck and shell the corn today. Jimbo, you and Charlie can help," Clive said.

"We were going fishing."

"Not now."

Nuben laughed at Jimbo's scowl and shook his head.

Served 'em right. Bo Jack put his six-year-old lips together and whistled as he ambled out of the barn.

The girls ran across the yard toward him, each holding berry pails.

"You buried those marbles. We can't find 'em. 'Sides that, Mama wants us to go berry picking. She needs some huckleberries and gooseberries for jam. Come on," Neva thrust a pail at him. "Mama's coming. She just tanned my hide for complaining."

He should have moved faster. Now he had to work, but the thought of those sweet berries made it bearable. Mama clambered down the porch steps and into the yard.

The Arkansas heat bore down on them as they walked close to the railroad track to the prime berry spot by Kokomo Creek. Halfway there, his sisters' steps slowed.

"Mama, it's too hot to be walking down here," Maye said.

"Why can't we do it later?" Neva said, kicking at the gravel beside the track.

"Girls, I'm not coming down here in the dark. You won't complain when we have jelly and jam this autumn."

"Can we eat some as we pick, Mama?" Bo Jack asked.

Mama laughed. She dropped his hand and hugged him close for a moment. "Yes, just fill up these pails first. I'm not wasting a trip."

In the end, Bo Jack felt sure they ate more than they picked, but the buckets remained as full as their bellies when they returned home.

He found Clive with his cousins still in the barn. They didn't stop shelling when he entered the corn crib. No, they ignored him past a greeting, so he decided to find something to play with. His uncle's hammer lay in the toolbox by the door. He grabbed it and pounded the sandy ground in the hallway of the barn. The soft ground gave way and the end of the hammer stuck in it. Bo Jack liked the slight resistance when pulling it out of the ground. He did it a couple more times.

His cousin Nuben came out of the corn crib just as he pulled it out again. "Boy, stop playing with that hammer. You'll hurt yourself."

Bo Jack ignored him and—just as Nuben disappeared back into the corn crib—hit the ground hard with the hammer. It stuck deep, so he yanked it with all his might, and as he did, the hammer head propelled out with ease and arched above his head. Ow! His whole body reverberated. He reached up to find the claw of the hammer stuck in the top of his head. Shock gripped him and he pulled it out without ceremony. Blood poured. His heart raced, but he couldn't tell his cousins and brother without getting in trouble.

He ran for his aunt's house. The barn sat between their two houses. His mama had gone to his aunt's after the berry picking. Swiping blood out of his eyes, Bo Jack tried to shake off the queasy feeling in his stomach. He pushed through the door.

His Mama's face went white when she saw him. Mama didn't like blood. "Oh, dear Lord, bless my boy." She peered at his aunt. "Take care of him."

Aunt Do didn't hesitate. She cleaned him and doctored him with some salve. His heart rate slowed, and he took a deep breath, wiping away tears he didn't know he'd cried.

"Now, Bo Jack, tell us how this happened," Mama said.

Bo Jack's mind raced. He'd be in trouble if he told them the truth, so he blurted out the next thought he had. "Nuben hit me with the hammer."

"What?" Aunt Do's voice rose.

Footsteps sounded on the porch. The door opened and there stood Clive and Nuben. Clive's eyes narrowed and Nuben's widened. "How dare you hit this boy with a hammer, Nuben. How could you do such a thing? You could have killed him." Aunt Do went at him like a hen on a biddy.

Nuben held up his hands. "Wait, Mama. I didn't hit him. He was playing with the hammer when I came out of the corn crib. I told him to stop or he'd hurt himself."

"Well, you should have taken it away from him."

Bo Jack dashed out of the kitchen before she could turn around. He'd had it for sure. Now his backside would hurt worse than his head.

His aunt caught him before he got off the porch. "Bo Jack, you come here to me," she said.

Bo Jack squeezed his eyes shut and turned, opening one eye first to test her level of anger. A stern but patient look met him. She raised her eyebrows and tilted her head until he opened his other eye. He swallowed hard and faced her.

"Why did you lie to me?"

"I knew he'd told me not to play with it and knew I'd be in trouble for disobeying."

"He's your older cousin, but he's not grown. Still, you should have listened to him. But, Bo Jack, accidents happen. Don't lie about it. No spanking for you today. You put hurt on yourself."

"But Clive—"

"No, he won't take the belt to you. You have my word. He's done his best by all of you since your daddy died, but there are times when I'll relieve him of that and let him just be your brother." Aunt Do brushed his sandy bangs off his forehead. "Your daddy, *my* brother, sure loved you. He hated getting sick. You would have loved him about now."

Bo Jack looked past her, finding his tall brother watching from the doorway. Clive came out onto the porch. His aunt didn't blink. "You heard me, Clive."

"Yes, ma'am," Clive said and then gazed down at Bo Jack, inspecting the top of his head. "That's gonna leave a scar, boy. Come on, I'm taking you to town with me."

Bo Jack couldn't believe it. He didn't get to go with his brother much. "Really?"

Clive laughed and scooped Bo Jack up, carrying him under one long arm as he went down the steps.

Bo Jack laughed, happiness dancing in his stomach. Clive set his feet on the ground and slung an arm around his shoulders. He turned his head to smile at his aunt on the porch. She waved, but Nuben had joined her. He glared at Bo Jack.

His cousin wouldn't forget.

Chapter Five

Neighbors, Soldiers, and Ice

The heat persisted as his sisters and cousins started a new school year the day after Labor Day. Bo Jack couldn't start until the next year. He stifled his boredom after morning chores by visiting Mr. Fenner. The old man and his wife lived close to the tracks not far from them. Boy, oh boy, could that man tell stories.

Mr. Fenner came out in the yard. "Where you headed, boy?"

Bo Jack shrugged and cocked his head to one side to look up at the man. "Around. How about you, sir?"

"Well, I'm glad you came by. You haven't been by much this summer. Man, let me tell you, I saw the biggest snake I've ever seen in my life. Aye, G— he was as big as a telephone pole and took down two rows of corn before I picked it. Then it went across the field and tore down Mr. Parker's fence. I'm surprised he didn't get into your uncle's field."

Bo Jack laughed. The old man could spin a tale, but he liked his stories.

Mr. Fenner gave him a mock serious look. "Laugh if you like. That was the biggest snake I ever seen. I need to go tell your aunt about this bird that came by the other day. Have you heard from any of your cousins since they left?"

Since the war started, his oldest cousins had gotten drafted. All of them had married before the war and didn't live at home, but close by. Thank goodness Gary got to stay stateside flying military transports for the US Army Air Corps, but Jigs served in the Navy, and Red landed in the Army infantry. Red had brought a friend home with him after basic training while on furlough. His friend came from New York City and had never seen a cow or horse.

"Only Red. We got a letter this week," Bo Jack said.

"I might have to stop by and have your aunt tell me his news." Mr. Fenner chuckled. "His Italian friend sure had a time on that cow Red had him ride. Well, I guess you'd better go on inside and see the missus. I think she has a piece of pie for you."

Bo Jack couldn't keep his smile from growing.

Mr. Fenner hooked his thumbs in his galluses. "Get on in there, boy."

"Yes, sir." He really liked that old man.

Mrs. Fenner greeted him with a hug. "I saved a big piece of lemon pie just for you."

"Thank you." He followed her into the kitchen. Their talks over pie covered everything from possum hunting to church meetings.

He emerged an hour later, full and happy, humming as he walked beside the railroad tracks. Those rails stayed busier these days, so he kept a safe distance. He kicked a few rocks and started to head home but turned back at the sound of the familiar rumble and whistle. Hands of young soldiers waved and they pressed their faces to the windows, smiling at him. Tears spurted to his eyes. He waved back, thinking of his three cousins.

Bo Jack loved them, especially Red. Aunt Do said he'd be serving with General Patton's Third Army. The news on the radio had mentioned that general, but Bo Jack just hoped he'd be nice to his cousin.

The train rumbled past. Bo Jack didn't move. He watched until the smoke disappeared and the whistle and rumble faded. A drip of sweat snaked its way into his eye and he blinked.

He couldn't wait for cooler weather. It brought to mind possum hunting. He'd about tired of fishing. Besides, his dog liked to go with him. That reminded him. He hadn't seen that dog all morning. Where'd he run off to? He broke into a run.

The yard stood empty. Mama had left to help a lady clean her house in town. It felt strange without his sisters and cousins. Today felt lonelier than before. The image of some of their times the past week brought a smile to his face. He chuckled.

His sisters and cousins had waited until after Mama left for work last week. They'd gathered in their kitchen to smoke coffee grounds. His cousins Tina and Jean had kept eyeing the door. Just as they started puffing, footsteps sounded on the porch.

"Someone's coming," Neva said.

Those girls spurted and stuffed the evidence in their pockets. They all jumped up and scrambled out the back door, heading for the woods. Bo Jack had run too but couldn't keep up with them. What if he got in trouble for it? So he'd run to the barn and ducked under the loose board. His dog had followed him. That mutt refused to go home with him when he left. The shady corner with the soft hay. Yep, that's where he'd be.

Bo Jack ran toward the barn. Sure enough. The young bird dog lifted his head at his approach but didn't bark.

"Hey, boy. You're getting lazy. Come on." The pup ignored him and resettled his head on his paws. Bo Jack laughed. Maybe the dog had it right.

"Well, it is right hot. At least a breeze is stirring in the hall here. I guess I could rest a bit." A yawn took him and Bo Jack settled beside his pup in the hay and slept. Cold weather had to come soon.

****

In a few months, the creeks and ponds froze over.

The weekend arrived, and Jimbo and Nuben came knocking early. Mama let them in and brought them to the kitchen to warm a bit.

"Can they go skating?" Jimbo asked.

"Skating?" Mama laughed. "None of you have any ice skates."

Nuben grinned. "We don't need none. Shoes will do on the pond."

"Please, Mama," Bo Jack said.

"Maye and I will take care of him," Neva said.

Mama's eyes gave each of them her look—the look—and they knew.

"Tina and Jean are outside waiting. We'll watch him, and his dog can even come," Jimbo said.

Mama sighed. She hugged Bo Jack. "You listen to them."

Excitement tingled. "Yes, ma'am."

A flurry of chaotic donning of coats and hats preceded the thunder of their trampling feet on the porch and down the steps.

Bo Jack's dog joined the group without the need for an invite. The girls giggled and struggled to keep their balance and footing. Jimbo and Nuben took to the ice with a few smooth slides to start. "Come on, Bo Jack," Jimbo called.

Bo Jack took a few tentative steps. He glanced back at his sisters and girl cousins laughing as they skated, holding hands at the pond's edge. They never did what Mama told them to do with him. He looked back at Jimbo. "Coming."

His dog whimpered and started to bark as Bo Jack inched his way to his cousin. The pup ran along the bank barking once he reached Jimbo and Nuben.

"I did it."

The barking stopped.

The girls screamed.

Jimbo grabbed Bo Jack and he slid, turning to look. His dog disappeared under the ice. No!

His eyes turned back to his cousins in desperation. "We got to get him."

"Whoa, Whoa—you'll drown or freeze if you try. I'm sorry, but he'll have to find his own way out," Jimbo said.

"But he'll drown." Bo Jack tried to pull away from his cousin, but the five-year age difference yielded Jimbo more strength.

"It's better him than you. Now come on—let's skate to the girls, and I'll show all of you some tricks," Nuben said.

Bo Jack's heart twisted, his eyes fixed on the broken ice at the edge, but he followed his cousins. The girls stood there with tears on their faces.

"We're sure sorry," Maye said.

Nuben left him and Jimbo with the girls and strode up on the bank by the trees. He drew back and started running. Just about the time he left the bank, he stumped his toe on a tree root and his momentum hurtled him toward the iced pond. He hit it headfirst and went all the way through.

Bo Jack could only stare—first his dog and now his cousin.

Jimbo, Tina, and Jean slipped and slid trying to reach their brother. The icy water churned and splashed. His cousin broke the surface. A strong swimmer, he waved his brother and sisters away, struggled out, and crawled back onto the bank. He pulled his pants off—they stood by themselves, frozen stiff.

A whimper sounded behind Bo Jack, and he turned to see his dog scrambling and belly crawling from his hole at the icy pond's edge. Neva raced to stand beside him.

"The others are taking Nuben home before he freezes to death. We'd better do the same for your dog. I don't know how either one of 'em got out of there, but Nuben said there was space under the ice—between the top of the water and the bottom of the ice."

Neva took off her coat.

"You'll freeze," he said.

"Not if we hurry."

They rushed over to his young dog and wrapped his sister's coat around him.

Maye ran ahead to their aunt's house. Aunt Do bolted out and hurried them inside before sending Maye to get Mama. Neva and Bo dashed up the steps, but Aunt Do stopped them at the door.

"You can't bring that dog in here."

Tears filled his eyes. "Please—just 'til he gets dry, and then I'll take him to the barn."

She sighed. "Just this once, but you have him out of here before Ernst gets home."

Neva smiled at him and they scurried inside.

Chapter Six

School, Nuben, and Girls

The day Bo Jack started school, Aunt Do sat him down on the porch for a talk before they left for the bus stop. He had just turned seven. His sisters and cousins waited for him outside.

"Now, when you get to school," Aunt Do said. "I don't want you to fight. I don't want you to start any fights. But don't you take nothing off those other kids. Because my boys—I always told 'em if they started a fight at school, they were gonna get it when they got home. So I don't want you to do that."

"Yes, ma'am."

Both she and Mama kissed his cheeks.

Mama walked him out on the porch and called out to his sisters who waited in the yard for him. "Y'all make sure your brother gets to class."

Bo Jack started off the porch to go to the bus stop with his sisters and two girl cousins who

47

waited with them, but Nuben stuck his head out from around the corner of the house.

"Come here." So Bo Jack went around to the side of the house. "What Mama told you is right, but—" Nuben said, "—if them little old girls give you any problems, you just kiss 'em."

Hm. Bo Jack studied his cousin's face. He didn't seem to be funning him, so he shrugged. "Okay. Thanks, Nuben."

Bo Jack left for the bus stop with a wealth of knowledge from his aunt and cousin. That and having his sisters with him took away his uncertainty about school. He found the bumpy bus ride exciting. Going to school might be fun.

The bus pulled up in front of the school. He followed his sisters off the bus. Just as he stepped onto the sidewalk, a bunch of girls his sisters knew and hadn't seen all summer descended on them. Neva and Maye hurried off with them. At least he still had Mary, or so he thought, but here came her best friend. They'd better not all leave him. He'd tell Mama. Mary grabbed a boy named Eddie when he got off the bus. He lived at Dixie Curve not far from them.

"Eddie," Mary said, "Would you be sure Bo Jack gets to his room all right?"

Eddie eyed him. "Yeah, sure."

Bo Jack frowned at Mary before she walked away with her friend. He turned back to find Eddie waiting for him.

"You ready?"

Bo Jack nodded. They'd nearly reached the building when Eddie ran into one of his friends.

"Hey, you told my sister—"

Eddie appeared confused for some reason but said, "Just go into that door down there and you'll find your room."

Bo Jack stared up at the big, cold building and got mad. Just wait until he told Mama. His sisters had not minded her, and she always gave him a whipping for not minding. Maybe he should just walk home. He checked the empty curb behind him. No, he didn't relish the idea of the two-mile walk.

He turned back to face the building, marched to the door and opened it. The dark hallway loomed in front of him and he hesitated. "No, I'm going home—'cause my sisters done wrong and they're in trouble, and I'm going to get them punished for not doing what Mama told them to do."

As Bo Jack closed the door, a woman strode down the hall with another little boy about his size. She had him by the hand and walked like Mama. He grinned. The boy's feet hit the pavement every other step.

Bo Jack figured the boy might be going to his same class. Maybe he should try. He stepped in the door and took off after them. The hall went down to a subfloor, and he followed them all the way to the classroom. The boy went in and Bo Jack stayed on his heels. The teacher seated the boy, so Bo Jack went to her. "Is this my class?"

"I believe so, young man," she said, "What is your name?"

He told her, but the same confused look he'd seen on Eddie's face appeared. "Please tell me again, just a little slower."

He tried three times and told her he had sisters at the school. Something must be wrong with her hearing. Why couldn't this woman understand him? One of the boys he recognized from church tugged on her sleeve and whispered in her ear. She turned back to him.

"I'm sending for your sister."

She led him to a desk. In a few minutes, Mary came in the door and gave the teacher his name and information. After Mary left, the teacher called him by his name. Bo Jack scratched his head. His family seemed to understand him just fine. He didn't get it.

The teacher was talking again, and he faced forward. The morning passed without further incident. He kind of liked the books they looked at and liked watching her write on the chalkboard. Still, when she announced recess, the whole class changed.

The tidy line of children became an unruly mass in the yard. A boy pushed Bo Jack, and he remembered what his aunt had said. Well, he didn't start it. The other boy had when he pushed him, so Bo Jack socked him in the nose. Blood spurted. Two buttons went flying off the boy's shirt during the scuffle.

Their teacher came running. "Bo Jack and Tony, you go to the restroom and get cleaned up right now. Bo Jack, you hold a towel under his nose until it stops bleeding."

In the course of things, Tony apologized for pushing him and Bo Jack apologized for bloodying his nose. They had made friends by the time they came back out, and they hit the playground talking.

Tony seemed to understand him okay, but some little girls teased him. He remembered what Nuben had told him, so he kissed both the girls.

The teacher came running. "We do not do that, young man. You go on back to the room and wait for the class there."

Bo Jack waited in the room, dreading more punishment.

The rest of the class trickled in after a few minutes, but the teacher didn't come with them. No one spoke to him. They returned to their desks except for one girl, one he didn't know. She jumped up in a chair and let loose a shrill shriek. Bo Jack laughed. *She's funny. I can scream louder than she can.* With that, he stood up on the chair and screamed just as the teacher walked into the room.

Oops, in trouble again.

"Bo Jack, put your head down and take a nap right now."

She chose napping as punishment? He suppressed a laugh, but after torturous minutes stretched into an hour of squirming over his desk without any success . . . she might not be so dumb.

The bell rang. He could not get to the bus fast enough. Once seated, he refused to talk to anyone. His nose stayed pressed against the window until the bus stopped.

They got off, and he ran over to his aunt's house to find everybody waiting on the porch to see how his day went. Well—he told them, then glanced at Nuben, who pulled his hat down over his eyes and peeked at Aunt Do. Bo Jack told about kissing the girls.

"Nuben, you may be 'bout grown, but I should tan you."

Everyone laughed, but Bo Jack knew Nuben liked to prank; besides he owed him for the hammer incident.

Chapter Seven

Fights, Police, and Dixie Curve

One night after dinner, yelling and screaming echoed through the air. Clive and Mama hurried to the door. Bo Jack and his sisters glanced at each other and scurried after them. As they stood in the front doorway, car lights shone close to the gravel road by the railroad tracks. Bo Jack made out the shadow of two figures. It sounded like men yelling at each other.

"Tarnation. They're going at it now. I'd better get the sheriff. No one go outside," Clive said.

The sound of grunts, fists, and metal followed. Mama made them get ready for bed.

Bo Jack ran over to his bed and plopped down on his belly to peer out the window. The sound of a siren droned and then stopped. The police arrived.

"Bo Jack, you get to sleep," Mama said from the doorway.

He tried to obey but lay staring at the dark ceiling. His brother's heavy footsteps pounded on the porch about twenty minutes later.

"Is everything taken care of?" Mama asked.

"Yes, ma'am. They'd been drinking. The fight was over some girl. She saw the whole thing from the car. One of 'em hit the other one in the head with a tire tool. Turns out that man is married and lives down at Dixie Curve. His wife won't be happy—he's going to jail." Clive chuckled. "Well, come to think of it, given the circumstances, she might."

"Clive," Mama said.

"Sorry, Mama."

A moment of silence followed before they both burst out laughing.

Bo Jack grinned in the darkness. He flipped on his side. Just wait 'til he told his friends about this. He thought about the man being from around the Dixie Curve. A lot of mischief happened around there at Halloween. They could get away with things then. The older boys had to let him go with them this time. What would they do this year? He'd find out in a couple of days, he thought, then drifted off to sleep.

The days shuffled along until Halloween night came. Jimbo and his friends, Eddie, Floyd, and Hutch, along with Bo Jack and Hutch's little brother, Davy, climbed into the corn crib to pocket some shell corn. They went down to the Dixie Curve by the main highway, cars passing them all the way.

Jimbo snickered and elbowed Hutch. Eddie chuckled.

"What's so funny?" Bo Jack asked, stopping.

"Yeah, what gives?" Davy came to a standstill beside him.

The older boys glanced back at them.

"Don't start giving us grief or we'll send you both home," Hutch said, but Jimbo turned and came back to them.

"You two had better listen to us and listen good. We can have fun if you do what we say. Are you game?" Bo Jack glanced at Davy, and then they both faced Jimbo and nodded.

Jimbo took some of the shell corn out of his pocket. Hutch joined him.

"When the next car comes along, we'll throw some corn at it. I'll go first, then you, Bo Jack, then Hutch, Eddie, Floyd, and Davy."

The sound of tires on pavement and the whirr of a motor signaled their first mark.

"Be casual—keep your hands in your pocket and stroll along. I'll bring up the rear."

His cousin's first toss hit the car's fender as it started around the curve. The driver slowed but didn't stop. They laughed when the car moved out of sight.

Bo Jack turned. "Here comes another one." His heart raced, and he switched places with his cousin. He threw the corn underhanded, up and out as high as he could. It rained on the top of the passing car. He got ready to run when the car slowed but calmed when the driver continued around the curve.

Hutch switched places with him when another car approached, going a bit faster. It didn't allow much time. Hutch gave a quick sideways toss toward the passenger side of the car. The sound of it hitting the window or metal didn't come, but the driver pulled over a few feet ahead of them. He jumped out of the car shouting. "Who hit me in the face with this corn?"

Hutch whispered, "His window must have been down. Get ready to run."

Then the man pulled out a gun. Tall Hutch grabbed Davy's hand and Jimbo took Bo Jack's. They ran. Shots rang out behind them. Davy hit a sweetgum sapling, but Hutch never slowed, dragging poor Davy right up that sapling and out the top of it. It got darker the further away from the road they ran. Eddie passed all of them. The sound of heavy breathing and running feet filled the darkness. Then a scream filled the air—Eddie's scream.

They ran toward it, but Eddie had kept going, leaving three broken, rusty barbed wires in the fence in front of them.

"Come on. We've got to keep running," Floyd said. He dashed through the broken fence and raced ahead, not waiting for them.

Bo Jack gasped for air.

"Keep up," Jimbo said, running in front of him.

Bo Jack's eyes had adjusted to the darkness by then and saw Floyd up ahead of them. Floyd looked back over his shoulder as they gained on him, but turned back. "Oof." Floyd hit the oak tree square. Hutch and Jimbo reached him first.

"He's out cold," Jimbo said.

Moaning emanated from the ground.

"No, he ain't," Hutch said. "Can you get up, Floyd?"

"You boys keep up. We'll have to help Floyd home and hope we find Eddie," Jimbo said.

When they neared Aunt Do's, Bo Jack broke off from the group. "I'm going home," he yelled.

"Don't you say nothing about nothing," Jimbo called.

Bo Jack slowed to a walk before reaching the back door. He leaned over with his hands on his knees, gulping for air until his chest relaxed and his breaths came easy. After one last look toward the road, he pushed open the door and slid inside.

Maye and Neva sat by the radio. Neva put her finger to her lips. "We're listening to the best part."

Bo Jack breathed a sigh of relief. No questions. His stomach rumbled and he headed for the kitchen.

Mama sat at the table with a glass of buttermilk. She smiled at him. "Did you have fun with the big boys?"

Bo Jack licked his dry lips. He didn't like lying to Mama, but it had been fun in a way.

"Yes, ma'am." His eyes scanned the clean kitchen, then he plopped into a chair. Mama slid her glass toward him.

"Could you finish this for me, son? I'm heading to bed." She scooted back her chair and stood.

"Yes, ma'am. Good night, Mama."

"Don't be long. Finish it and get to bed. Good night."

That buttermilk hit the spot.

The next day, Jimbo came by to get him early. They made the rounds checking on the other boys.

Eddie had cut his throat, his stomach, and his thighs on the barbed wire. He couldn't turn his head much either way. They found Floyd with his eyes swollen shut and with a nose so swollen it almost covered his face. They ran into Hutch and Davy, coming out of Floyd's. Davy walked up to them straddled-legged because his riding out that sapling had rubbed the skin out from between his legs.

Silence ensued on their walk home. Then Jimbo started whistling. Bo Jack tilted his head, appraising his cousin with a sideways glance.

"We sure got lucky, Bo Jack," Jimbo said, glancing down at him.

"Sure did."

Chapter Eight

Sisters, Brooms, and Rocks

Even though Mama had work in other people's homes, she enforced spring cleaning in theirs. Bo Jack woke to the delightful sound of birds singing outside the window by his bed on a sunny Saturday morning. He stretched and yawned, relishing in the possibilities of the day.

"Bo Jack, you'd better get out of that bed," Mama said, opening the bedroom door.

She smiled while he finished stretching but pulled the covers off and pointed toward the door. "Get dressed and go to the outhouse. There's a bit of breakfast for you in the kitchen. Even though it's Saturday, I'm leaving for work. Your sisters are home today to do the cleaning, and you're going to stay here and help them."

Bo Jack made a face, but she lifted her eyebrow. Time to stop. No more protests. "Yes, ma'am."

She kissed the top of his head as he donned his pants. Before he had time to put on his shirt, she'd scurried out the front door.

He shuffled out the back door to the outhouse, ignoring his sisters' giggling. His contemplation and dread multiplied with the consideration of all they'd need to do to clean the six-room house. A slow shuffle back to the house delayed the inevitable for a few minutes, but once he opened the door, his sisters helped him to recount the rooms.

"Bo Jack, you're dawdling. We've got too much work to do for any of that. Here, take this rag and start dusting," Mary said.

Dusting—anything but that. He backed away, then took off running, but they chased him. He circled, sliding through the closest doorway, passed three bedrooms on one side, dodged through the kitchen then back through the dining room, and out the living room door.

During his second pass through the rooms, Neva yelled, "Head him off. He's coming through the kitchen."

A broom swooped by him, but he tucked his bottom and scooted past. He reached the living room and ran outside and rounded the house to the other side. His heart raced and he leaned over, putting his hands on his knees, gasping for breath.

"Fine. We won't let you back in for the rest of the day. Just wait until we tell Mama," Maye called.

Oh, no, Mama would tan him for sure. He ran to the back door—locked. "Let me in. I'll help."

No response.

He ran to the front door—locked. He beat on the door with his fists. Giggles emanated from the other side, but no footsteps approached to unlock it. Bo Jack plopped down on the front steps, and his dog came up to him, whining. "Hey, boy. They won't let me in."

Soft brown eyes understood, and a slow tail wag shifted his mood. So, what if they wouldn't let him help now. He didn't want to clean anyway. Bo Jack stood and ambled down the steps. "Come on, boy. We'll go play at Billy's." His pet barked. "Race ya." Boy and dog took off down the road.

He found Billie sitting in a fork of a tree in front of his house.

"Come on up, Bo Jack."

Bo Jack scrambled up to the limb next to Billy's. "Hey, you want to shoot rocks at the barn with me? My sisters locked me out of the house."

"Sure."

Billy jumped off the low limb to the ground below. Bo Jack followed his lead. "Want to race?"

Billy took off running in response, and Bo Jack and his dog rushed to catch up and pass him. They reached Uncle Ernst's barn in a dead heat, touching the back of the barn at the same time.

"Tie."

They ran over to the pump for a drink, then strolled to the end of the hog lot where a pretty good-sized tree stood. Its branches formed a fork in the top. Some time ago, he and Jimbo had climbed up and cut that tree fork off at each side. They'd tied some car inner tubes together, secured them to the stubs of the tree fork, and made a bean shooter.

Bo Jack kicked around the base of the tree where the strings and leather strap attached to the inner tubes dangled from it.

"Get as many rocks as you can carry in your pockets, and we'll shoot them."

After a few minutes of search and find, they pulled down the inner-tube pea shooter.

"You think we can do this without your cousin? Last time it took all of us pulling it."

"Yeah, we can do it. These rocks aren't as heavy as the ones he got us."

They worked together and situated the first smooth rock in the middle of the makeshift slingshot, pulling back together and releasing it like a catapult. The rock traveled all the way to the top of the barn.

"See? I told you we could do it." Bo Jack grinned and reached into his pocket for another rock.

They passed about an hour depleting their supply.

Billy rubbed his stomach after they finished. "I'm hungry. You want to go to my house for lunch?"

Bo Jack nodded and called his dog to follow. They spent the rest of the day at Billy's. When Bo Jack saw Billy's father coming up the road, he headed home.

A little guilt stirred in his gut. He crossed the railroad tracks, gathering the speed of a freight train by the time his feet hit the porch steps. Bo Jack gave the doorknob a tentative turn and found it unlocked. The mixed aroma of dinner cooking and the smell of mopped floors greeted his nose.

Mary came out of the kitchen.

"You go wash up. Mama and Clive will be home any minute. You'd better hope Mama makes it home before Clive."

Bo Jack gulped, hung his head, and headed out back to the pump. Once back inside, he sat on the edge of the overstuffed chair in the living room—waiting.

The front door opened. Neva and Maye's voices mingled in their rush to greet their mother.

"Mama, Bo Jack left home this morning, and he didn't help us do anything."

He closed his eyes tight at the purposeful sound of his mother's footsteps.

"Bo Jack, is this true? Look at me."

He stood, opening his eyes. "Yes, ma'am, but they locked me—"

"I don't want to hear any excuses. I told you to help them. Wait here."

His mother fetched the belt and took him by the hand. The whipping dance began. As he tried to outrun the belt in a circular pattern of evade and swat, Neva stuck her head out from around the doorway leading to the first bedroom and made a face at him. Maye giggled behind her. Mary must still be in the kitchen. At least she didn't laugh at him.

He thought of his dog's sweet brown eyes as the belt made contact with his bottom. Yep—dogs beat sisters any day.

Chapter Nine

War's End and a Plane Ride

Bo Jack sprang out of the bed after a night of hit-and-miss sleep. A mixture of fear and excitement had kept his mind churning the whole night. He'd mulled over the events of the last few months. The years of war had ended. Gary had completed his military duty and come home from serving with the Army Air Corps ready to open his own small airstrip. Today, Gary planned to take Aunt Do and Bo Jack for a plane ride. Bo Jack donned his clothes and even put on his shoes without being told.

In an odd moment, his sisters seemed excited for him. Mary kissed him on the top of the head and told him to hold on tight. Neva and Maye made him promise to remember every detail so he could tell them about it when they got home.

Mama finished clearing the breakfast dishes, removed her apron, and took his hands in hers. She looked down at him. "Are you sure you want to do this?"

"Yes, ma'am."

"You didn't like the first plane you saw."

He pulled himself up straight. "I was little then."

Mama laughed and nodded, patting his shoulder.

A knock sounded at the door. He dashed and pulled it open. Aunt Do stood there smiling. His uncle waited for them in the car.

"Good morning. Are you ready?"

He nodded. Mama came up behind him, kissed him on the head, and waved them out the door.

"Take good care of him, Do."

"You know he's like one of my own."

He ran down the steps ahead of his aunt and opened the car door for her. This earned him a pleased smile before he jumped into the back seat.

Getting to the airfield seemed to take forever. Bo Jack scooted to the edge of his seat and leaned forward with his arms propped on the back of the front seat.

"Boy, you're breathing down my neck. Sit back," his uncle said.

"Yes, sir."

Bo Jack slumped back in the seat but couldn't help kicking his feet a bit.

"Ernst, we'd better get there soon or this boy is going to jar the car apart," Aunt Do said, laughing.

The dirt airstrip and the metal hanger building came into view. Bo Jack pressed his nose against the window, watching a plane take off. Uncle Ernst parked and Gary came out. His tall cousin looked impressive in his flight jacket.

Bo Jack jumped out as soon as his cousin opened the door.

"Which one is it, Gary?"

Uncle Ernst shook his head. "You are a brave man, son. Taking this one up could prove more than you bargained for. Anyway, how long will you be?"

"I'll just give him a parachute if he gets out of hand." Gary winked at Bo Jack and turned back to his dad. "We can't stay up long—about half an hour. If you've got to go to town, I can give them a look at my other plane after we land."

"That's fine. I'll be back to fetch you, Do."

His aunt nodded and waved. Uncle Ernst climbed back in the car and pulled away. She walked over to Bo Jack and took his hand. "We're ready, right?"

If she could do it, so could he. Bo Jack swallowed, a flash of apprehension threatening to replace the excitement dancing within.

"Let's go," Gary said, whistling as he led them toward the waiting plane.

The interior of the small aircraft boasted little more than a pilot's seat for his cousin and a board seat just big enough for two behind it. Gary helped Aunt Do in first and then Bo Jack.

While they waited for Gary to do a final check of the plane, Bo Jack scooted closer to his aunt. He might be nine now, but still— "Everyone said to hold tight when we take off. Can I hold tight to you?" he asked.

She smiled down at him, and he took her arm. "Why don't we hold tight to each other?"

The pilot door opened, and Gary settled into his seat. He checked his radio and controls and then turned to smile at them. "Ready?"

"Yes, sir."

"Take us up easy, son. No showing off."

Gary wriggled his eyebrows and Bo Jack laughed. Aunt Do shook her head and joined them.

A man on the ground gave his cousin some hand signals, gave the propeller a spin, and the plane spurted to life. They started to move. His respect for his cousin grew as he picked up speed on the dirt runway and lifted into the sky. Bo Jack's stomach felt like it had stayed on the ground for a few minutes before it caught up with them.

As they leveled, he looked out the window. *Wow.* He turned back to gape at Aunt Do. "We're really high, huh?"

She smiled.

He scooted up toward the back of his cousin's seat, watching out the front. "You got to do this every day in the Army, Gary?"

"I did—just not in this plane. I had to fly bigger ones to transport cargo. Flying is what I want to do forever. Do you think you might want to learn? You know I took Red up and taught him a bit."

"Why didn't he join the Air Corps?"

"We all got drafted. He served in the infantry with General Patton. Remember?" Gary tilted his head a bit.

His aunt pulled him back beside her and pointed out the window. "You look down there and see what you can make out from here. I want to count the clouds."

"Everything looks too small to see real good. Can I count clouds with you?"

She laughed. "You bet."

He lost count when Gary tilted the plane, making a fun circle.

Aunt Do grabbed her hat.

"Do that again, Gary," Bo Jack said, squealing.

"Don't you dare, son."

Gary straightened the plane and turned to wink at them. "Yes, ma'am. Straight flying from here on out, Mama."

Bo Jack lost his stomach again during the descent to the airstrip. Aunt Do whispered a prayer, but Gary landed as smooth as a boat floating on a still pond.

"Don't move until I stop, Bo Jack," Gary said.

Once the plane halted, his cousin climbed out and came around to open their door. He helped Aunt Do first and then Bo Jack.

"Golly, Gary. Can I go up again with you?"

Gary laughed and threw his arm around him as they walked toward the hangar. "Not today, but I'll take you up some more. I'll be giving flying lessons here. When you're older, you might want to get your license."

"Don't be putting ideas in his head," Aunt Do said.

Gary grinned.

Bo Jack spotted the other plane as they neared the hangar. He pulled away from his cousin and ran ahead. "What's this one, Gary? Does it work?"

"It's like some of the ones I flew when I first started military transports stateside. It still needs work, but you can have a look." His cousin opened the plane door and lifted Bo Jack inside. "Look around, but be careful. I'll—"

"Hello, Mama."

Gary turned and Bo Jack poked his head out of the plane as Red entered the hangar. Aunt Do hugged her second oldest son—only two years separated Gary and Red. Six years separated Gary and Jigs. It struck Bo Jack how close Nuben had been to being in the war with the slim two years between them. But of all the brothers who'd served, Bo Jack could see the biggest change in Red.

Ever since returning, he'd been around Aunt Do's house more and checked on all of them. He'd seen him talking to Clive several times. Whereas, before the war, being married, he'd spent most of his time with his wife and her family. Bo Jack liked Red's wife, and he loved Red.

Red straightened from hugging his mother and slapped Gary on the shoulder. "You need to let me take one of your planes to see our uncle in Texas."

Gary nodded. "Just as soon as you finish training with me and get your license."

"We'll work on that. Ginny might have my hide." Red elbowed Bo Jack out of the way and climbed onto the plane with him. "What do you think of it?"

"It's nifty, but I liked the one Gary flew us in this morning better." A thought struck Bo Jack. "Hey, Red, you want to go out with us on Halloween?"

Gary laughed. "What? I'm not invited?"

"Sure you are, Gary."

Aunt Do shook her head. "I think they've had their share of Halloween-night mischief, and after last year and the year before that, I'd think you had too, Bo Jack."

Red grinned at him. "Why? What happened?"

Giddiness filled him. Last year had been more fun than the previous year. "Well, the first year they took me, a man shot at us—"

Red's grin faded.

Aunt Do cleared her throat.

"Not at us, but in the air. We thought he was going to shoot us for throwing seed corn at his car. Everyone got injured racing out of there but Jimbo and me. Boy, were we lucky. Anyway, this past year we opted for mud balls instead. We—"

"The law came after you for hitting that patrolman's car," Aunt Do said.

Shock reverberated and Bo Jack blurted, "How'd you find out? He didn't catch us. We ran up to the cafe."

His aunt laughed, Gary ran a hand through his hair, and Red pulled him in front of him within the confines of the plane.

"I think I've had enough action for now. You be careful. But if you ever need me, I'll come."

Bo Jack stared at his cousin's face, noting the light creases on his brow.

"Red, they said you fired the first shot after crossing the Rhine River. Did you?"

Red let go of his shoulders and wiped his nose with the back of his hand, glancing away and then back. "I don't remember that, but I fired too many shots. I pulled this big gun on a truck and had it ready to turn and fire for our battles. That's all I remember." Red ducked his head and exited the plane. "Come on out here, boy. Daddy sent me to get you and Mama. He got tied up getting the wood from the mill."

Bo Jack sensed a mixture of tension and sadness in his cousin, so he didn't protest. Instead, he climbed out and hugged Gary, thanking him for the ride and the tour before following his aunt and Red to the truck.

Chapter Ten

A Bicycle, Indians, and Swimming Holes

The months rolled by past Halloween. They'd scaled back this year, only using a stuffed dummy in the road to scare some guys into thinking they'd hit an actual person. Now on to Christmas—one of the happiest for Bo Jack and his sisters, thanks to his cousin. Red made sure they had oranges, apples, and a few presents.

A new rhythm intermingled with the everyday one in the postwar world. The absence of loved ones who would never return trailed in the shadows of those rejoining life stateside. Optimism glowed in the embers of many still living in sacrifice and poverty. That summer, a dream of Bo Jack's materialized.

He'd been gone all day fishing and swimming with his friends. The time had gotten away from him and he headed home after dark. Clive would tan him for sure. He ran toward the house, but something metal caught his eye in the bright moonlight. A bicycle sat in the front yard. Where had it come from? It had a flat tire, so maybe someone had left it there and planned to come back for it later. But who? He glanced at the front window on the house—a lamp still burned.

Clive must be waiting up for him. Shoot. Bo Jack didn't want a spanking. Maybe if he waited until the kerosene lamp went out, he could sneak in without anyone knowing. About ten minutes later, the light went out, and he waited another few creeping minutes before he opened the door as quiet as he could.

Bo Jack sighed in relief and slid into bed. He flipped on his side but froze at the sound of Clive's voice.

"Mama, is that the boy?"

He peered across the room where his mother slept—or so he'd thought.

"Mama, don't tell him it's me. Don't tell him it's me," he said.

He flattened when she ignored his pleas and answered his brother. "Yes, it's him."

"Boy, come in here."

Bo Jack swallowed hard before sliding out of bed. He squared his shoulders and went to Clive's bedroom.

Clive took his belt and tore up Bo Jack's little backside. Strange, but thoughts of the bicycle distracted him while Clive spanked him. It didn't seem to hurt too much. Once finished, Clive didn't say anything. He put away his belt and climbed back into bed.

Bo Jack ran back to Mama. "Mama, I took my spanking. Sorry I let it get late. Whose bicycle is that in the yard?"

She sighed in the darkness. "You need to get home before dark. Don't make your brother have to spank you again. Is that understood?"

"Yes, ma'am. What about the bike, Mama?"

"Red brought it by for you earlier. You'll have to fix the flat and everything. He brought you some tube-patching stuff to help."

"It's mine? Really?"

"Boy, you get to bed, or I'll be giving that bike back to Red," Clive said from the other room.

"Yes, sir."

Bo Jack willed sleep to come, but he tossed all night in his excitement. He'd wanted his own bike for so long.

The next morning, he skipped breakfast and ran out to inspect his bike in the daylight. He'd never worked on one, but he tore off the flat tire and glued a patch on the tube within minutes. Once he reattached the tire, he pushed it about half a mile or better down the gravel road to the little store by the Dixie Curve and put air in it. His hands shook as he climbed on his bicycle. *His* bicycle. He'd ridden his friends' bikes from time to time but had never thought he'd ever have one of his own. Boy, did he love Red.

The wind ruffled his hair and swooshed in his ears. Nobody could tell him anything today. Just wait until his friends saw it. He'd show Howie and Billy first.

Howie wasn't home, but he found Billy fishing at the creek.

"Whose bike is that?" Billy asked.

"Mine."

"Stop fibbing."

"I'm not. Red got it for me."

Billy pulled his empty hook from the water and laid his pole aside. "Really? Can I ride it?"

A wave of selfishness spiraled within Bo Jack at first, but he remembered Billy had let him ride his bike last year before he wrecked it. Bo Jack hesitated. "You promise to be careful?"

"Sure, I just want to try it."

Billy kept his word. He rode it in a broad circle a couple of times and returned it. "It's great. You want to fight Indians today?"

They'd found some change in the street last weekend and had seen the latest shoot-em-up movie at the show.

"Sure."

They fought about five hundred or more and could see another thousand running toward them in the next couple of hours.

"I'm out of ammunition. You got any?" Billy asked.

"Only what's in my rifle here." He pretended to shoot a few more times. "I'm out. We'll have to fight 'em hand to hand."

Bo Jack battled his imaginary adversary with all his might. Billy did the same until he slipped on the pine straw.

"Oh, he got me," Billy said.

"I'll save you."

Bo Jack turned and grabbed Billy's hand, but his friend moaned when he tried to stand.

"I think my ankle's broke or something."

Bo Jack released his friend's hand and ran for his bicycle. He rolled it over to where Billy sat on the ground.

"You've got to get on my bike, and then I can push you to the road."

After a struggle under Billy's bigger size, they managed to get him on Bo Jack's bike. He pushed Billy all the way to the highway and then doubled back to get him home.

Billy's mother sat on the porch shelling peas. She rushed down the steps. "Bo Jack, go to the field and get Ben."

Billy's dad ran back to the house with him. Once Billy's parents had him in their car, Bo Jack headed home. Good thing he'd had his bike. Poor Billy could have more accidents than anyone he knew. He'd broken his wrist last year jumping near a cable by the swimming hole.

Swimming sure sounded good. He'd bet he'd find Howie and his brother at the Blue Hole or Railey's hole. As long as he watched the time, he could show them his bike and cool off a bit before heading home.

Bo Jack remembered when his cousins took him to the Ouachita last year and taught him to swim close to the bridge. They'd had fun until discovering the town sewage had leaked into it that day. There were too many other swimming holes to choose from to put up with that. They'd left and went to Railey's. Maybe, Jimbo and his friends would be there today. He missed his cousin.

Once Jimbo had started high school last year, he didn't want to play much. Neither did Neva and Maye. He rolled his eyes thinking about them primping and talking about boys. Girls—who needed 'em? Except Mary. She'd graduated last year and left home for a chance to model in New York. Maybe there'd be a letter this week.

Laughter and splashing drew his attention near Railey's. Only boys swam there as none of them could afford swimsuits. Bo Jack scanned the faces bobbing in the water.

"Hey, Howie."

A hand waved back from the group treading water.

"Where'd you get the bike?"

"Red give it to me."

"Wow. You swimming?"

"Yeah—"

"Girls coming." Ken, Howie's brother, hollered from the bank.

A mass exodus took place from the swimming hole. Boys scrambled onto the bank, grabbing clothes and dressing. Ken must be the designated lookout today. Some of the teenaged boys had started bringing their girlfriends to swim on rare occasions. What a nuisance. That had happened yesterday. Now they'd have to sit around on the banks and wait for them to finish swimming. He could almost see the steam coming out of his friends' ears.

"Well, aren't you sweet to let us have the water to ourselves," one of the two girls said, giggling as they topped the bank.

"Why don't you boys try the Blue Hole today or Social Hill?" Steve, one of his cousin's friends, said, following his girlfriend toward the water.

They all wore swimsuits and had towels slung over their arms. My, my, wasn't that nice.

Howie and Ken finished dressing and ambled over to him.

"Nice bike," Ken said.

"Thanks. I let Billy ride it."

"Did he wreck it?" Howie asked.

"Nah, but he did break his ankle or something when we were playing. I got him home though."

Howie shook his head. "Sounds right. We'll check on him tomorrow."

"You want to go to the Blue Hole?" Bo Jack asked.

"Nah, we got to get home. We did chores early, but Daddy said he wanted us home by lunch."

Chores! He'd plum forgot.

"Yeah." He peered up at the sun straight overhead. "Guess it is time for lunch."

His friends waved and turned toward the road.

"See ya," he said, hoping Clive and Uncle Ernst weren't waiting for him.

He rode as fast as his legs could peddle. His legs burned after he stood up to pull the hills. Just when his lungs felt ready to burst, gravity pulled him down the other side where he coasted on the breeze.

Aunt Do and Uncle Ernst's house came into view. Bo Jack braked and put his feet on the ground, slid off his seat, and gripped the handlebars. He stood there for a moment. Dread filled him. He swallowed hard. Time to take his medicine. He put his right foot on one pedal and slid onto the seat, placing his left foot on the other pedal as he started off again.

"Bo Jack, wait up."

Bo Jack wobbled a bit when he turned to look over his shoulder. He braked and hopped off his seat again as Jimbo ran toward him.

The damp ends of his cousin's hair told Bo Jack where he'd been. "How was the Blue Hole?"

Jimbo grinned. "Great. The splash from the rope swing never gets old." He walked around Bo Jack's bike. "Like it?"

"You knew about it?"

"Of course I did. Red wanted to surprise you."

"He sure did."

"I see you fixed the tire. Have you been riding all morning?"

Bo Jack tucked his chin. "Yeah."

Jimbo stopped in front of him. "Hey." His cousin gave his shoulder a gentle shove. "What's wrong?"

Bo Jack squelched the impending tears but not the words. "I was so excited about the bike this morning—fixed the tire and got the air—and forgot all about chores. They'll tan me again and take my bike away."

Jimbo laughed.

Bo Jack didn't know whether to be angry or relieved, so he just stood there.

"We made it without you this morning. Everyone knew about the bike. No one's gonna say anything. Just thank Red and all will be well. In fact, just telling him about your morning will be thanks enough. Now, quit moping and head to the house. I'm starving after swimming. Bet you can't catch me."

Relief mixed with the elation of a challenge, propelling him back onto his bike. He stayed on his long-legged cousin's heels until they entered the yard and then passed Jimbo right before they reached the barn.

"Whoop—Red picked you a good one. Lean it by the barn and let's eat," Jimbo said, grinning.

Bo Jack secured his bike and walked back to where his cousin waited.

Jimbo lifted an eyebrow. "Beat you to the porch."

They took off in an even run, but his older cousin beat him with ease. "That makes us even."

Bo Jack nodded and laughed, following Jimbo into the house. They found the kitchen empty, but his aunt had left lunch and a note for them on the table. Being Saturday, schedules could vary. Turned out, Aunt Do and Uncle Ernst had gone to town for a few things and planned to go by Red's afterward.

"Looks like we are on our own," Jimbo said, taking a napkin-covered plate and a glass of milk to the table.

Bo Jack followed suit.

"Aren't you hanging out with friends this afternoon?"

Jimbo picked up his fork and shoveled peas into his mouth. He chewed and shrugged. "A few of the guys may swing by later. It's too hot to do much in this July heat." He took a drink of his milk. "How about you?"

"Billy broke his ankle this morning. Howie and Ken had to get home." Bo Jack couldn't believe his cousin might hang out with him again. He didn't want to jinx it though, so he just grinned and picked up his fork.

They ate in companionable silence and then washed up their dishes and headed outside.

"Want to try my bike?" Bo Jack asked.

Jumbo grinned but shook his head. "I'm a bit big for it, but thanks."

Bo Jack smiled but caught movement out of the corner of his eye. He turned. Hutch and Davy were veering off the road, coming toward them.

Jimbo elbowed him and hollered, "Wanna have a corncob fight?"

"Sure," Hutch called back.

"Bo Jack and me against you and Davy. Every man must find his own cobs and hiding places," Jimbo said when their friends joined them.

Hutch and Davy ran for the corn crib where they kept the fresh shelled cobs, but Jimbo motioned for Bo Jack to follow him. Jimbo headed for the hog pen and Bo Jack understood his intent.

Bo Jack and Jimbo hurried to gather the wet, heavy cobs left from the hog's slop. He followed Jimbo back to the barn. They rounded the corner.

Bo Jack glanced up at the outside door that they kept closed to keep the rain out and elbowed Jimbo. "Look up there."

Davy had cracked the door and was sitting up there, watching them.

"I'm going to hit him through that crack," Jimbo said.

"Yeah, right," Bo Jack said.

Jimbo threw one of the heavy, soggy cobs. Bo Jack's mouth fell open as he watched it travel straight through the crack.

Davy hollered.

"You hit him," Bo Jack said, half thrilled and half mortified.

Jimbo's face went white. "I didn't think I could hit him. It should have hit the barn."

They stared at each other for another suspended moment before they took off to the barn in tandem. When they reached the barn hallway, they found Hutch helping his injured brother down.

"Really, Jimbo? You could have blinded him?"

Blood poured from the gash just under Davy's eye.

"I'm sorry, Davy. I never thought I could hit you from there," Jimbo said.

"Fat help that is," Davy mumbled. "I'm gonna have a shiner."

"You kept your eye, though," Bo Jack said and then wished he hadn't when Hutch glared at him.

"Let's get him cleaned up and go fishing," Jimbo said.

Davy winced but grinned. He headed to the pump with Hutch.

"We'll just say the other guy looks worse," Davy said.

"You got it," Jimbo said.

Bo Jack sighed in relief. This had turned into one of the best days in a long time. He had a bike of his own and got to spend time with Jimbo and his friends. "I'll go dig some worms and get the poles," he said.

Chapter Eleven

Friends and Fires

The break of dawn brought them to work in the fields, the noon sun burned at the day's pinnacle, and toppled them into swimming holes for a respite in the afternoons. Most days didn't want for activities, but as the summer days stretched toward August, pockets of boredom emerged.

Bo Jack didn't even feel like riding his bike today. He kicked the gravel beside the railroad tracks and headed for Howie's and Ken's house. Before he reached their yard, they ran out to meet him.

"Where ya headed?" Howie asked.

"To see you."

"Nothing to do here," Ken said. "Want to go to the store with us?"

"Sure, but I don't have any money. Why are you going?"

Howie grinned at his brother but only shrugged.

Bo Jack didn't care about why, so he nodded, and they ambled down the road.

The heat beat down on them the nearer they got to the store. Bo Jack's mouth watered at the sight of a man taking a cold bottle of soda pop out of the box beside the door. He didn't linger—no sense wanting what he couldn't have. The old screen door creaked and slammed behind them as they entered.

Howie and Ken dashed to the counter.

"Hello, Mr. Sanders. Daddy needs some matches," Howie said.

Bo Jack stood behind them. Why didn't he believe Howie? He kept quiet and watched the brothers complete the transaction with Mr. Sanders. They turned and grinned at him, motioning for him to follow.

Once outside, he asked the question burning inside him. "Why'd you really buy those matches, Howie?"

Ken laughed. Howie smirked and leaned against the trunk of the car parked outside the store. "We're gonna have some fun in the woods."

Bo Jack scratched at an insect bite on his neck, contemplating this. "Why?"

"Just because," Ken said. "You in?"

Something quivered deep in his gut, but he squelched it. "Sure."

Howie took off running and Ken and Bo Jack followed him to the woods close to Mr. Hugh's house, about a quarter of a mile from their house. They stopped at the edge, where the tree line met the field. The wind whipped through the trees, shaking the branches and stirring the leaves. Howie ducked under a couple of tree limbs. He glanced up and moved to a gap in the trees. Howie took the matches from his pocket.

"Hey, what are y'all doing?"

Howie almost dropped the matchbox. Another school friend joined them.

"Jess, don't sneak up on people."

"I didn't sneak; I walked up on you. There's a difference," Jess said.

"Never mind. We're gonna throw some matches down and stomp 'em out quick."

"It's hot enough."

Howie shook his head. "We're just doing it for fun and won't let them burn long."

"Oh," Jess said.

Howie returned to his task. He slid open the matchbox and removed four matches. He handed one to each of them. "I'll go first."

Howie struck his. Bo Jack and Ken huddled by him to block the wind. The dry leaves crumpled into flames without delay and they stomped them out, but Jess hadn't stayed with them. Instead, while they stomped, he scrambled to another gap in the trees a few yards away and started his own fire.

"You'd better watch yours, Jess. The wind's blowing—we can't let them get out of hand," Howie said.

"I won't."

They turned back and Ken struck his match and threw it down. Bo Jack's heart raced and they stomped out the flames. The trees stirred above them.

Bo Jack eyed the rustling leaves. The treetops beside him bent and swayed a bit. That something deep in his gut stirred again. He looked at his friends. Ken's eyes widened. Jess screamed.

They turned.

"Help."

The gust of wind had spread their friend's small fire away from him. Jess stomped and kicked dirt, but the flames had burned to the edge of woods. They froze as another gust of wind lifted the flames in a spiral of ash and leaves, spreading flames toward the field.

Jess ran toward them. "What are we going to do?"

"Run," Howie instructed them.

Each one ducked and dove their way through the foliage to the road, not daring to cross the open field in plain sight. They ran behind old Mr. Fenner's house and on to Howie and Ken's house. The brothers dashed in the barn, but Jess ran toward his house, and Bo Jack took off running toward the lumber company. He passed it, crossed the railroad tracks and cut through the fields, climbing fences that obstructed his progress. As he circled back and neared Aunt Do's, he met Jimbo and Nuben.

"Whoa, whoa—where you been?" Nuben asked.

Fear gripped Bo Jack's innards. He tried to swallow, but he had no spit.

"I've been playing, but we heard there was a fire. See," he said, pointing in front of him to where smoke rose in the sky.

Jimbo's eyes narrowed, but Nuben took him by the arm.

"We'd better go see if we can help. Bo Jack, go get Daddy. He can fetch Red, Gary, and Jiggs. Clive's still at the mill."

Guilt pulled at him, but he couldn't betray his friends. So he ran for help as fast as he could.

After his uncle's truck disappeared down the road, Bo Jack sought a cool place beside his dog under the house. He didn't want to be forced to fib to the girls right now. So, he waited. It seemed time had stopped. Every second dragged longer than the one before. His dog gave him a disgruntled look and crawled out to the yard. He followed him.

"I don't blame you," he said, bending to rub the dog's floppy ear before he headed for his climbing tree. Bo Jack scrambled to the first forked branch. He squinted at the sky. The clench in his gut eased a bit when he saw a mere wisp of smoke.

"Supper time," Mama called.

Maybe time hadn't stopped. Still, he didn't feel hungry.

"Boy, you'd better get down out of that tree. Don't you hear Mama calling?"

Bo Jack's stomach jumped. Clive stood at the base of the tree with his arms crossed. His mouth went dry. "Yes, sir. When did you get home?"

Clive shook his head, and Bo Jack climbed down, scraping his big toe on a broken twig. He hopped on one foot for a minute in order to check his injured toe. Clear—no splinter.

His brother stood there with his arms crossed, waiting.

Bo Jack headed around back to wash his face and hands at the water pump. Clive did the same, and then they headed in the back door.

Maye and Neva set the serving bowls on the table and slid into their seats.

"There you both are," Mama said, placing the bread on the table.

Bo Jack pulled out his chair beside Neva.

"Where have you been off to today?" she asked.

"Just around," he mumbled.

"Let's say the blessing," Mama said.

Clive made quick work of the task and reached for the bowl of okra. He talked as he spooned some on his plate. "Did you hear about the fire, Mama?"

Bo Jack held his breath.

"No. I've been inside. Where was it?"

"Close. Behind Mr. Hugh's place. It almost reached his house. I ran into Uncle Ernst and the boys on my way home. Seems like it started in the woods behind his field."

"The field with his crops or the other one?"

"The other one. That's the good thing."

"Do they know how it started?" Maye asked, taking the bowl Clive passed her.

Mama took a piece of bread and handed the platter to Clive. Bo Jack shook his head when Neva offered him the okra.

"Well, they found part of a match, so someone was in those woods. They just don't know who," Clive said.

"Evermore," Mama said. "Why would someone take matches into the woods in this heat?"

Bo Jack took a slice of bread and kept his chin down. He glanced up when his brother didn't answer Mama. Clive's eyes met his for a brief instant. He held his breath.

"No one is sure, but they think it must have been some kids playing around. The sheriff questioned Mr. Sanders at the store. He said some kids had bought some matches today, but the store was busy, and he couldn't recall exactly who they were."

"Well, I bet the sheriff is going to find out. Those rascals need to be held accountable," Mama said.

"I agree, but as it didn't reach his house, Mr. Hugh is going to let it go this time. He said he'd planned on burning that field due to ticks anyway."

"Yes, but he didn't plan on burning the woods. He would have had men present to keep it contained until after the next rain," Mama said.

"True, but the wind moved it toward the field, and they got to it in time to prevent it from reaching more than the trees right inside the edge of the woods. They didn't find any dead animals."

Dead animals. Bo Jack put down his bread. He'd never even thought about that possibility. Tears spurted from his eyes, so he grabbed his glass of milk and gulped a swallow.

"So, the sheriff isn't going to push this?" Mama asked.

"No, Mr. Hugh said his house and crop field are safe, and that's what matters to him. But Red told me the sheriff wants the boys in this area to go by and help Mr. Hugh put up a new fence. That way all of them can see the damage. It might prevent something like this in the future, as well as give the boys responsible a chance to pay Mr. Hugh back a bit without anyone knowing who they are."

Neva handed Bo Jack a bowl of corn. He took it and put a small spoonful on his plate.

"That includes you, Bo Jack," Clive said.

Bo Jack's head lifted. "Yes, sir. When?"

"Tomorrow is Saturday. Uncle Ernst doesn't need you then. You go in the morning. If Mr. Hugh doesn't want you to help, he'll send you home."

"Yes, sir."

"Good. Now, finish your supper. The fights are on the radio tonight."

Maye and Neva moaned. Mama smiled at them. "Your brother has been working hard. Let our boys have the radio tonight."

Bo Jack wanted to slip away and go to bed, but squelched the urge. He couldn't believe he'd followed Howie and Ken into this mess. If Clive knew—they didn't have the money to pay for a field or damages—but that's just what Clive and Mama would have insisted on doing, not to mention the other punishments all of them could have faced. Mr. Hugh had prevented such consequences. Bo Jack wouldn't forget it. No, he never wanted to even hold another match for as long as he lived.

Chapter 12

Moping and Roping

Bo Jack never forgot about that fire. After helping Mr. Hugh on Saturday, he vowed never to follow anyone else's lead again. He couldn't shake his remorse.

Jimbo found him on the porch steps moping after church on Sunday. "Hey, it's time you learned to ride and rope without a saddle. Nuben showed me, and we can use his cow horse, the one he trained for the rodeo. Come on."

Bo Jack heaved a sigh and stood.

Jimbo slung an arm around his shoulders but didn't say anything on the way to the barn to get the horse. His cousin grabbed a lariat rope before escorting the bridled but bareback horse to the pasture where a calf stood by his mother.

"Help me flush the calf into the next field," Jimbo said, securing the horse next to the fence.

Bo Jack ran and undid the barbed-wire gate in the fence separating the two fields. He slipped the looped wire from around the end post, walking the gate a good distance back before spreading it flat on the ground. He and Jimbo worked as swingmen to round up the calf and run him into the field. Bo Jack ran back, picked up the gate, and put it back into place, closing the gap before the mother cow could join her young one.

Jimbo ducked between the strands of barbed wire next to where the horse stood. He walked him around to the metal gate at the front of the field and slid it open. "You can sit on the gate and watch first."

Bo Jack climbed to his perch. Jimbo now sat on the bareback horse facing him, holding the lariat rope. The calf stood on his cousin's left, eyeing his mother on the other side of the fence to Jimbo's right. His cousin readied the rope, and the calf broke and ran. The horse backed his ears and took off after the calf. Jimbo swirled the rope over his head in an impressive show. The calf veered back to the left, and his cousin followed in swift pursuit.

"Get him, Jimbo," Bo Jack hollered.

The calf made a sudden dart to the right. The horse turned—right behind him, but Jimbo went straight, bypassed the horse's head and flew into mid-air, still swinging the rope. He tipped forward with the rope still in motion all the way to the ground.

Bo Jack laughed and couldn't stop. His insides hurt and he struggled to breathe. He half fell off the gate and leaned against it until he could take in some air. "That's the funniest thing I've ever seen," he said, walking toward his motionless cousin.

Wait.

Bo Jack broke into a run, sliding the last few feet like a baseball player to home plate.

"Jimbo," He shook his cousin's arm.

After a moment, Jimbo lifted his head, moaning. Skin hung and gaped from his jaw and cheek on one side of his face. He still clutched the rope.

"Can you move?" Bo Jack asked.

Jimbo released the rope and pushed up on his hands and knees. He shook his head and moaned again.

"I'll go get Uncle Ernst." Bo Jack hurried to his feet.

"No. Daddy don't need to come. Just help me back to the house. Mama will get me cleaned up in no time."

Bo Jack struggled to get his teenage cousin to his feet. As they started toward the gate, Nuben came running across the yard, followed by his sisters. They'd seen the whole thing from the porch.

"We've got him," Jean said, sliding her arm around Jimbo's waist.

Bo Jack stepped back and Tina took his place, flanking her brother on the opposite side from Jean.

"We'll finish the lesson another day," Jimbo called back to him.

"No, I'll teach him later," Nuben said. "Looks like you might need another lesson to boot."

Bo Jack ran back and retrieved the lariat rope. Nuben joined him in the field before he reached the gate.

"Help me get this calf back to his mama. Then you head home. I'll get my horse."

They repeated the wire gate and round-up routine, returning the calf within minutes. Nuben looped the wire over the post, stopped, and chuckled.

Bo Jack turned his head to the side and squinted at him. "What?"

"He did look pretty funny flying through the air."

"Yeah, he did." Bo Jack could still see it plain.

A fresh round of laughter circled between them. Nuben's horse trotted up to him and nickered.

"You did good, boy—staying on the calf, that is."

Nuben patted the horse's neck and gathered the reins.

"I'll head home," Bo Jack said.

"Hey, are you starting fourth grade this year?" Nuben winked at him. "No, your days playing hooky last year ruined that."

Bo Jack ducked his head and kicked at the dirt. Why did Nuben have to remind him?

"Yeah, yeah—I'm back in third again. That teacher bored me."

"If it's the same one this year, hang in there, or—" Nuben grinned. "you can always kiss her."

Bo Jack wrinkled his nose and shook his head. "Nothing doing."

Nuben chuckled.

Bo Jack shoved his hands in his pockets and turned for the road. He neared the back of the house but found he didn't want to go inside. Instead he circled around to the front and got his bicycle. The front tire appeared a little low. He'd take it to the station near the Dixie Curve to put some air in it. Everything closed on Sundays, but the air hose stayed open and free for anyone who needed it.

The road was quiet and open all the way to the curve. He might ride over to the Blue Hole after he got the air or maybe go gigging frogs or bagging fish at the mill pond. Maybe Billy could go with him.

Nary a soul appeared at the service station. A quick swipe removed the sweat running down his face. He climbed on his bike and stood up on his pedals to get momentum and then resumed his seat when he'd gained a steady speed coming around the curve.

He leaned, a rush of warm wind brushing his face, and moved into the straightaway. As he did, a black winged visitor flew by and landed on his neck. A flurry of hit-and-pull initiated and ended in hit-away-and-panic as he glimpsed its small ears—a bat.

He dislodged it and dodged the winged visitor's last attempt to land on his person. His bike wobbled and slid into the gravel at the edge of the road. A quick adjustment of balance and application of brakes saved him from wrecking. His heart thudded. Did it bite him? He rubbed his neck with his hand and used his fingers for a finer examination but didn't find any blood on them or feel any sore.

Maybe he should have Aunt Do have a look. Mama didn't like to see him injured. Besides, he really should check on Jimbo.

Bo Jack straddle-walked it back to the road. A quick check found it still deserted. He pedaled as fast as he could.

By nightfall, his aunt had deemed both him and Jimbo fine. Uncle Ernst educated him on the fine insect-eating points of bats versus his aunt's caution because of disease. Thank goodness the critter hadn't bitten him, but it had scared him.

Chapter Thirteen
Transitions and Tragedy

Bo Jack's third grade rewind started taut and unfurled fast. He sped through it, as well as fourth grade. The slow days of childhood intertwined with the new speed of Maye and Neva's teenage years.

It seemed they lived more at school with activities with their friends than at home. He rolled his eyes every time a boy knocked on the door. Maye put everyone at ease and chatted without any awkward pauses. However, a reserved shyness had overtaken Neva and, though older, she often insisted on double dating with Maye and her beaus. Bo Jack missed his impish and mischievous sisters of old but knew they still loved him. They'd sometimes take an afternoon with him, even if just to walk and talk along the road by the train tracks.

The wind of change turned cold once it reached Aunt Do's. Uncle Ernst got sick— something with his throat. He had holes in his neck. Bo Jack couldn't understand how this happened. The adults called it cancer.

He watched in powerless sadness as his uncle faded away and died—the only father figure he'd ever known besides his oldest brother. His heart twisted and cried during these dark days. He had no words to help his aunt and cousins. Mama, Clive, and his sisters did what they could.

Jake came home for a few days, but Bo Jack didn't see much of him during his visit. Mama said his brother had business to tend to in town. He left without fanfare.

Mama and Clive worked hard. His brother grew quieter and his smiles became rare. Bo Jack never thought about his brother's age. Nuben dated one of Clive's old girlfriends, and Clive didn't seem to go out much anymore. He just worked.

Bo Jack bumped into his brother as he ran into the house before supper.

"Get on in here, boy. Mama and I have to talk to you and the girls," Clive said.

Bo Jack joined his sisters at the set table. Mama placed the bread beside him and took her seat. Clive pulled out his chair, slid onto it, and cleared his throat.

"Times are changing. We will be moving into a house in town. You girls are close to finishing school, leaving home, and probably getting married."

Bo Jack saw the twitch of his sisters' lips, but they knew not to interrupt Clive.

Their brother continued, "When that happens, I will leave the rest of the boy's raising to Mama. I want to go to California. Anyway, Jake has found us a house in town. I've written Aggy and Mary. They responded and agree this is for the best. Since Mama doesn't drive, she won't have to walk as far to work or to town when she needs something. The house question is settled. We have sold this house and will take you by the other one tomorrow. The move will be in two weeks."

Bo Jack licked his dry lips and stared at his sisters. He found them smiling. "But what about Aunt Do?" he asked.

Clive glanced at Mama, and she shook her head. His brother's serious eyes met his. "She will be fine. Nuben is getting married. After graduation, Jimbo and his girl will do the same. There's rumblings in world affairs. He might have to go in the military. Jigs, Gary, and Red have families of their own, but they will help as needed. The girls will be with her until they get married. We appreciate all they've done since Daddy died, but I stayed home in hopes of getting you raised, so Mama could handle things. It's getting close to that time. This move is part of getting there."

"What about my friends and my bike?"

Clive gave him one of his rare smiles. The girls and Mama laughed. Bo Jack crossed his arms and ducked his head.

"Put your chin up. Your friends go to school with you, so they get to town. They might like coming to our house there. What an adventure. You'll need your bike to get around. One day, you might get a job throwing papers," Mama said.

Bo Jack lifted his head and grinned. He'd never thought of that. It might be fun to live in town. Then another thought struck him. "Mama, can we come visit Aunt Do every week?"

This time Mama didn't look at his brother. Her eyes stopped sparkling and filled with tears. "No. It's too far to walk or ride your bike from our new house."

"But Clive will drive to the mill to work. I can come with him and see Aunt Do."

Clive cleared his throat. "The mill may be reducing jobs or closing. I'm not sure how long I'll be coming out here. You've got school."

"But could I come this summer?"

Neva squeezed his hand under the table.

"Maybe James and I could bring him in June," Maye said.

Bo Jack liked Maye's boyfriend just fine but didn't know why he'd be seeing his sister in the summer.

"I'm sure James will have more important things to do after graduation," Clive said.

Mama shook her head. She swiped at her eyes. "I'm sure we can get somebody to drive us if Clive is gone. You children forget your Aunt Do and I grew up playing together long before her brother took a shine to me. She's a friend who became my sister-in-law. As none of us have telephones, it might be nice to have a visit by summer."

"That's settled. Let's eat," Clive said, picking up his fork.

But Mama bowed her head and he put it down again.

Neva squeezed Bo Jack's hand. He tucked his chin and closed his eyes. His stomach growled as Mama blessed their food.

Bo Jack glanced up and Mama reached for the bowl of peas and passed it to him.

"How would you like to go to the brush arbor meeting this week, Bo Jack? It starts tomorrow night. The First Baptist church is hosting it down here. Charlie's mother said you can ride your bike over with him every night. She's helping out at the meetings."

"You mean meetings under that structure they build out of limbs and branches for church meetings outside—like that one at the end of last summer?"

"Yes."

"I don't know, Mama. I went to one with Billy last year. He went down front there and started talking funny. He said he got saved."

"That's wonderful. That's the very reason we have walked to church every Sunday we could. I hope you're ready one day." She peered around the table. "I hope that for all of my children."

Clive cleared his throat, and the girls ducked their heads.

Bo Jack invited them to the brush arbor meeting, but they laughed and begged off going. So Bo Jack rode over to Charlie's the next night, and they headed for the meeting.

They slid into the brush arbor and sat in the back right after the singing started. Something stirred in Bo Jack during that first meeting. It squeezed his heart, but he fought it. By the third night, Charlie squirmed in his seat beside him. "What's the matter?"

Charlie wiped his eyes and shook his head.

By the end of the meeting the next night, Bo Jack sat gripping the chair back in front of him. He gasped to breathe as they exited the tent.

Charlie grabbed him by the shoulder. "You're fighting it too. Do you think we need to get saved?"

Bo Jack ducked his head. "Maybe."

They didn't talk much the rest of the way home. But both stood in the same state at the end of the next meeting. This time, Charlie stepped into the aisle and Bo Jack stayed on his heels all the way to the front. Charlie's mother met them there with smiles and tears. She led them to the Lord. Bo Jack wept and didn't care who saw him. He wished Mama could have been there, but maybe she could be there for their baptisms.

Two weeks later, Mama witnessed his baptism at the First Baptist church. He had hoped they'd take them to the river, but the church now had a baptistry. Still, either place, his heart had changed.

Chapter Fourteen

Traffic, Lignite Mine, and Summer Farewells

"Do you think we can get a coke, Bo Jack?"

"Maybe. I found some dimes by the curb this morning. But we need to reach the cafe first."

Bo Jack stood up on his pedals, trying to keep them steady and compensate for his friend's weight behind him as he pulled against the gravity of the hill. Davy sat on the luggage carrier, gripping Bo Jack's waist to keep from falling. Sweat poured down his face even as a cool autumn breeze caressed it.

"The game was exciting today. That Charlie can sure throw a football," Davy said.

"Uh huh. Hang on a minute, Davy," he said. Bo Jack approached downtown, watching the lights.

"There's Officer Gibson on the corner," Davy said.

Bo Jack concentrated on the green light and went through the intersection.

An unexpected impact sent him straight up in the air and threw Davy clear. A car moved below him and his bike slid under it. Time suspended and everything slowed. Wham! Time resumed and he landed with a jolt in the street. "Oof!"

Bo Jack turned his head. Davy pushed up off the street and dusted off his pants. Bo Jack took a breath and did the same.

"Are you boys hurt?" Officer Gibson said, laughing and rushing to them.

"No," Bo Jack said.

Davy shook his head.

Officer Gibson turned toward the man who had hit them. He stood behind his car staring at Bo Jack's twisted bicycle.

His bike. Bo Jack's stomach churned. He'd be on foot now for sure.

"Stay here, boys. We will get this settled," the policeman said.

They waited, watching the man and Officer Gibson talk. In a minute, the men walked back to them.

"I am sorry, son, but I didn't see you when I turned. I'll pay to have your bike fixed. Are you sure you're not hurt?"

Davy shook his head.

Bo Jack twisted his arm around to see his skinned elbow and then bent it to wipe the trickling blood on his shirt. "I'm fine except for this little scrape."

The man's anxious face relaxed a bit. He reached for the pencil in his pocket. "Who's your daddy? Give me his number and I'll call him."

The words slapped Bo Jack's heart for a second. It must have shown. Officer Gibson put his hand on his shoulder and turned to the man. "Hold on a minute. I need you to write down your information for my report. His family will see how much it will cost to fix the bike, and we'll let you know."

The man nodded and took the writing pad from the officer.

"You boys hold on a minute and I'll see you home," Officer Gibson said.

They dropped Davy off first. His dad stormed into the yard with a flushed face. The policeman explained the incident and the man shook his hand. Davy waved before he went in the house.

Clive stopped working on the front door hinge and walked toward the car outside their new house.

"Did you know we have indoor plumbing and electricity at this house?" Bo Jack asked the policeman.

Officer Gibson stopped the car and smiled at him. "Really? You have truly moved up town."

Pride lifted the corners of his mouth. "Yes, sir. We don't need an outhouse, either."

Clive reached them. Unlike Davy's dad, his brother's face didn't even hint at his reaction. He opened the door on Bo Jack's side.

"Bo Jack, you go on in the house and let me talk to your brother," Officer Gibson said.

"Yes, sir."

Bo Jack didn't dare smile at his brother. He glanced at his twisted bicycle in the back seat and scurried past Clive to the side door of the house instead of the front. Mama opened it before he could.

"I ain't in trouble, Mama. A man hit Davy and me with his car."

Mama's face went white, and she pulled him inside the kitchen.

"We're fine. I just got skinned up a mite. The man's gonna pay to fix my bike."

She hugged him to her until he squirmed away.

"Are Neva and Maye home?"

Mama put her hands on her hips. "Don't you beat all? You scared the life out of me. No, they haven't made it home yet."

He slid into a chair at the table. Boredom set in fast. "I hope they get my bike fixed quick."

Mama laughed.

"It's not funny, Mama."

Clive opened the door and came inside. He went to the kitchen sink and washed his hands. "I'm taking your bike down to the bicycle shop. If it can be fixed, we'll see how much it'll cost. Officer Gibson said the man will come and pay the bill once we know."

After drying his hands on the dish towel, Clive joined him at the table. "Are you sure you're not hurt?"

Bo Jack lifted his elbow. "Just this. I'm fine."

"Good. Do you want to walk that hunk of twisted metal to the bicycle shop with me?"

"You bet." He jumped up, nearly knocking the chair over, and Mama laughed. Clive shook his head and stood. "Mama, we'll be back in a little bit."

Bo Jack hurried out the side door and circled around to his broken bicycle. Clive had leaned it against the front step.

He'd been lucky. Someone had to be watching out for him. So he planned to be even more careful once he got his bike back. He grinned at his brother. "Clive, there's no way I ever want to have another wreck like that."

"Well, that one wasn't your fault. Still, you'd better be careful. I don't want to hear of another one, either. Come on." Clive picked up the bike. "Let's see how long you'll be without it."

****

Bo Jack had it back within two weeks. The frame wasn't straight like before, but he could still ride it. The weather turned cold and forced him to put it away until spring. By then, he counted each day until summer break.

Mama had written Aunt Do about coming to visit. Neva had talked to Jimbo at school before graduation. He planned to marry his girl. Aunt Do wanted Bo Jack to come stay with her over the summer and Mama agreed if she could visit with Aunt Do the first day.

Clive and his best friend drove them. Bo Jack thought they'd never get there. He didn't know how much he had missed his old home until the railroad tracks came into sight. The new house might have plumbing and the new wringer washer Jake had sent to Mama, but it didn't have the memories and childhood adventures. He pressed his nose against the window.

Mama laughed.

The man who had bought their house waved as they turned right to go to Aunt Do's. It felt odd seeing somebody else there, but he kept quiet and scooted to the edge of his seat, looking through the windshield for Aunt Do on the porch. "Where is she, Mama?"

"Bo Jack, she has no way of knowing what time we're coming for sure. It's too hot to be on the porch. I'll bet she's watching out the window though."

Clive's friend drove into the empty front yard. The lack of activity hurt Bo Jack's heart. He studied the closed barn door. Nothing seemed right—not the way he'd imagined. Clive climbed out and helped Mama out on the opposite side, but Bo Jack stayed put until . . . Aunt Do.

She'd opened the screen door and waited on the porch. The sight of her face brought everything back. Bo Jack beat Mama up the steps and flung his arms around her ample waist. Aunt Do gathered him against her and kissed his head. "This can't be my Bo Jack," she said. "You have grown like a weed, child."

He stepped back and straightened, grinning. "I'm almost as tall as you, Aunt Do." The affection in her smile went straight to his heart.

"You sure are," she said and then turned to hug Mama. "Living in town agrees with you."

"It does, Do. We've come a long way. I never thought either one of us would end up living in town."

Aunt Do laughed. "No, I did good to get you to stay in the house instead of under it as a child."

"What? Mama got under the house?" Clive asked, grinning as he came up the steps with Bo Jack's suitcase and handed it to him.

Bo Jack grasped it with two hands on the handle.

Mama shook her head. "You boys don't be listening to this nonsense."

"Nonsense is right. That's what it was, plain and simple. She went under there and no one could get her out except me. I had to crawl up under there. Do you even remember why you did it?" Aunt Do said.

"No," Mama said, laughing. "I'm surprised your brother even considered me."

Aunt Do took Mama's hands in hers. "He adored you." Mama's eyes took on a faraway look and she blinked. Bo Jack hoped she wouldn't cry.

Clive ambled back down the steps and headed to the car where his friend waited. He untied Bo Jack's bicycle from the back and leaned it against the porch steps.

"You be careful, boy. Mama, we'll be back for you before suppertime."

Bo Jack shifted his hold on his suitcase to one hand and waved as the car drove away. He turned back toward the house, and Aunt Do smiled at him.

"I have an early lunch ready for us. Then you need to go see Billy. He's come by here three times since school let out, asking when you were coming. I think he plans on you two going to the Lignite Mine swimming or one of those swimming holes. Today is a good day to do that. Your mama and I can have a nice visit."

After lunch, a knock sounded on the door. Bo Jack opened it to find Billy standing there grinning.

"Hey."

"Hey. Hang on a minute," Bo Jack said and ran back to hug Mama. "Billy's here."

"Have fun. Now, you mind your aunt and we will be back for you in August. Remember, you're supposed to talk to the man at the paper about getting a route."

"Yes, ma'am." He turned to his aunt. "I'll be back before nightfall."

Bo Jack didn't wait for a response and ran out the door. He found Billy standing by his bike where Clive had leaned it.

"No, Billy. You have to ride in back of me. Clive will have my hide if I wreck this again."

"Ah, come on, Bo Jack. I ain't gonna wreck it."

It would be easier for Billy to double him as he still outweighed Bo Jack, but— "No, maybe on the way back. We'll see. Aunt Do said you might want to go to the Lignite Mine?"

"Yeah, that water is sure clear where they dug all that lignite out of it. Besides," Billy said, walking over to the tree. He turned with a twenty-two rifle in hand. "I want to do some target practice."

"It ain't loaded, is it?"

"No, I've got the shells here." He patted the front pocket of his overalls. "I can lay it across my lap."

Bo Jack shrugged and straddled his bicycle, waiting for Billy to climb on the back.

Billy held the rifle in one hand until he got situated and then put it across his lap.

"Ready?"

"Ready."

Bo Jack teetered a bit, and Billy didn't say anything, but then, as they wobbled down the road, going a little to the left and then a little to the right, his friend cleared his throat.

"What's wrong with your bike?"

Bo Jack dared to turn his head to flash a brief grin at his friend. He turned forward to keep them in the road. "Well, it's been hit by two cars. The first time was after a football game before Halloween and then last month, I got hit again."

"How?"

"Well, I had just come out of seeing the matinee movie—you know the shoot 'em up show. Anyway, after I saw it, I pretended my bike was a horse. As I neared the place where Davy and I got hit, another car hit me. I flew up in the air and landed on the street, skidding backwards. Good thing I kept my head up or I would have hit it on the curb. The second man was from out of town. Aggy's husband had to get him to pay the repair bill."

The bike shimmied toward the old log road.

"They didn't fix it too good. The frame's warped," Billy said, his voice reverberating with the vibration beneath them.

Bo Jack kept quiet and concentrated on navigating the dried mud road. As they neared the dug-out mine, he exhaled the built-up air in his lungs. "Looks like only a couple of people are here." He coasted to a spot by a rock and released the kickstand. Billy crawled off and scrambled down the incline to the clear water.

"Come on. First one in gets to pilot your bike on the way home."

Bo Jack hurried to follow him, but Billy reached the edge first.

"Cannon ball."

His stocky friend splashed into the water with a tidal wave in his wake. Bo Jack ducked his head against the wet onslaught. Billy surfaced and hooted his triumph.

"I'll teach you how to ride that bike right."

A spark of irritation rankled Bo Jack. He jumped off the edge, pulling his knees up and splashed to the right of his friend. The water cooled his sweaty skin. His head broke the water's surface. He spit and shook dripping water from his eyes while treading water.

"You want to go to the creek and get some crawdads after this?" Billy asked, swimming over to him.

"Sure, but I'm doubling you."

Billy sent a spray of water his way. "Aww, come on, Bo Jack. I don't have accidents like I used to. Besides, I'm bigger than you. I can double you on a bike easier. Just look how hard you had to work to get us here."

His friend had a point. "You'd better promise me—'cause Clive will tan me sure. I'm supposed to start a paper route when school starts. I need my bike."

Billy grinned and drew a quick X across his chest with his finger. "Cross my heart." He treaded in a circle. "Race ya."

Bo Jack made a quick frog kick and then settled into fast swim strokes to overtake his friend before they reached the other side. They repeated the race back across, and Billy took him that time. After about an hour, a few other boys joined them, and it became too crowded to race or do tricks off the sides.

They scrambled up the slick rocks and made their way to Bo Jack's bike. Billy grabbed the handlebars and straddled the frame, keeping it steady for Bo Jack to climb onto the back rack with Billy's rifle across his lap. Bo Jack put one hand on his friend's shoulder to steady himself.

"Ready. Now, remember your promise. Don't go too fast."

Billy turned his head and grinned as he started pedaling toward the dried mud road. They approached the hill leading to the road.

"I go fast, but I get there," Billy said, taking off down the hill.

Bo Jack's stomach stayed at the top and had just caught up with him when the bike began to shimmy. About halfway down the hill, signs of where a dual truck had come through after the rain last week remained. The prints of the tires showed the point between the dual tires in the dried, pressed mud. Billy fought to control the warped bicycle on the uneven terrain, and Bo Jack held on tight.

Billy got the front wheel on one side of the apexed mud and the rear wheel on the other side.

He fought to steer, but oversteered and ran up onto the edge of the road where the gravel started.

Bo Jack's right leg caught on a bush, dragging him off the bicycle. He landed in the middle of the road on top of Billy's twenty-two. He lifted his head to find Billy and his bike.

Billy fought the bike the rest of the way down the hill and wrecked it in the creek below.

Bo Jack wrinkled his nose and turned his head to the side as he cringed. Yep—just as he'd thought. He jumped up, picked the gravel from his palms, and grabbed the twenty-two. Good thing it wasn't loaded.

Billy had picked himself up and waited for him on the edge of the creek. "I'll get Daddy to fix your bike, but I think we can still ride it home."

"I'm doubling you."

Billy gave him a sheepish grin. "You are." He leaned the twisted bike against a bush. "Hey, since we're by the creek, let's get some crawdads before we head home."

"Sure. I ain't in no hurry to get back on that bike just yet."

They laughed and commenced the crawdad search.

Two hours later, Billy and his father brought Bo Jack back to Aunt Do's with his semi-repaired bike in tow. She met them in the yard.

"What did your brother tell you?"

"It wasn't his fault, ma'am. I wrecked it," Billy said. Bo Jack sent him a grateful smile.

Billy's dad pushed the bike to Aunt Do. "It's rideable, but barely. I did what I could. Tell Clive

I'll keep my eye out for a better one for the boy. He tells me he's going to work delivering papers."

"That's what they tell me. I'll let Clive know. Thank you."

Billy waved as they drove away, and Bo Jack waved back.

"Come on up here on the porch and let's have a chat. I might listen better with a little dip of snuff."

So, Aunt Do got a little dip while Bo Jack told her about the wreck. She nodded every now and again but didn't say anything until he finished. "I'm glad they picked up your mother before you came back. Otherwise, they might not have let you stay the summer."

Bo Jack gulped. Surely not. "Aunt Do, I won't play with Billy anymore this summer."

She chuckled and shook her head, rocking a bit faster. "Now don't be making rash promises. Of course, you'll play with him. You can't stay under my feet the whole time. Just next time, don't take the bike, and maybe go to the Blue Hole to swim instead, or even Rockport."

"No, not Rockport. The last time we did that, we got leeches."

"Don't you want to find the outlaw's cave over there?" Aunt Do said with a twinkle in her eye.

"I don't believe it. Jimbo and his friends never found it—or so they said. They wouldn't let us go with them."

"You never know."

"No, I'll pick the Blue Hole. It's cool and fun. Besides, the creek runs next to it in case we want to gig some frogs or get more crawdads. We caught some for Billy's mother today."

"Sounds good." Aunt Do stopped rocking and stood. "Let's go in and play cards. It's time you learned the game of Pitch. You can help me with chores tomorrow."

The house seemed so empty without his cousins and uncle, but his aunt's laughter joined his and filled the void. They played until suppertime, then ate, and listened to a radio show for a bit before bedtime.

He hugged his aunt tight and crawled in bed satisfied, but contentment gave way to contemplation in the fight to sleep. Everyone had grown up except for him. He rolled over on his stomach and stared out the open window. A warm night breeze blew through the screen and the night song of frogs, katydids, and cicadas drifted on it. At least Maye had one more year at home with them. Neva had a job waiting for her in a nearby town and would be gone by the time he returned home. He couldn't even imagine Clive leaving but knew the time approached.

Aggy, Jake, and Mary leaving first had taught him to let go. The same went for his cousins. They still loved him, and he'd see them sometimes. Just wait until he could drive. He'd visit everyone no matter where they went. You bet he would. Too bad they didn't let people visit from heaven. He'd like to talk to Uncle Ernst and his daddy.

Slumber captured him with heavy eyes and yawns. He flipped on his back and fell asleep, with the timeless summer sounds, winds, and sweet grassy smells of his childhood home soothing him for one more summer.

Chapter Fifteen

Papers, Punches, and New Friends

Bo Jack parked his bike outside the small building on time, but he found the door locked. How did Mr. Jenkins expect him to get his papers rolled and delivered on time? He went around to the back and found a window halfway opened. After a moment's hesitation, he slid through it.

"Well, looky here." A boy about his age emerged from the shadows of the dim building, flanked by two others. The trio sized him up for a moment in silence.

Bo Jack kept his eye on the one who had spoken. Sandy-haired, wiry, and slim. A few years shy of being a hoodlum but well on his way. The youth had a toothpick between his teeth and a rolled-up newspaper under his arm.

Whack. The rolled-up newspaper hit Bo Jack before he even saw the guy move.

Aunt Do's advice from long ago flashed— never start a fight, but don't back away. Bo Jack knocked his opponent to the ground and straddled him.

"Get him, Skip," One of the other boys said.

Skip squirmed beneath him and stretched back to reach a nearby cane chair. Bo Jack braced to block the crash aimed at him,

"Break it up," Mr. Jenkins dove into the fray, grabbing the chair from Skip's grasp.

Bo Jack unpinned Skip and sprang to his feet.

Their boss flipped on the lights and turned to them with his arms crossed. "What's the meaning of this?"

"That kid snuck in the window on us," Skip said.

Mr. Jenkins lifted an eyebrow. "And how did the rest of you get in this morning?"

"The window—but we know each other. We don't know him."

"This is Bo Jack. Now you know him. Bo Jack, these ruffians are Skip, Lowell, and Dump. I'm sorry to be late this morning. Although I prefer you to wait for me in the future, I do appreciate you getting started. So stop wasting time fighting and finish rolling and bagging the papers. I want your saddlebags loaded and on the back of your bikes within a half an hour."

Bo Jack kept his mouth shut and got to work. He had his bags packed first and took them out to his bike. The other boys' bikes leaned against the front of the building. They sure had shiny chrome and straight frames. Much better than his. No matter—he'd get the job done.

He pulled the slip of paper listing his route from his pocket and double-checked his papers in the bags behind him, then took off down the street. Mr. Jenkins had driven him along his route the previous afternoon. Nerves and adrenaline mixed as he pedaled in front of his first house, reached back for a paper, and let it fly toward the front doorstep. He held his breath until it landed on target. His bike wobbled, but Bo Jack grinned and reached back for another paper.

Once he found his rhythm, he finished his route with ease and headed back to report to Mr. Jenkins. He noted the absence of the other bicycles in front of the building and started to whistle. So, he'd done it—finished ahead of the rest on his first day and delivered two-hundred fourteen papers. He steered to the side of the building and coasted to a stop. Bo Jack removed the empty newspaper bags from the back of his bike and headed inside. He found Mr. Jenkins in his office. The door stood open, but Bo Jack still knocked. "Excuse me, sir."

Mr. Jenkins looked up from the paperwork on his desk and glanced at his watch. "Are you finished?"

Bo Jack held up his empty saddlebags. "Yes, sir."

His boss smiled and folded his hands in front of him on the desk. "That's real fine. Good job. You just might work out, that is, if you can stay out of trouble with the other boys."

"I'm here to do my job, sir. If they don't bother me, I won't bother them."

Mr. Jenkins nodded and stood. He circled around to the front of the desk. "They can be a little rough around the edges, but they're good workers. Do you think you might make friends with them?"

"That's up to them. I didn't start that fight this morning."

"I see," Mr. Jenkins said. He rubbed his nose and glanced toward the front door.

Bo Jack turned as the other boys entered, jostling each other and laughing. They pulled up short when they reached the doorway of Mr. Jenkins' office.

"Routes finished without breaking any milk bottles this morning, boys?"

"Yes, sir," Lowell said.

Skip and Dump nodded.

"Good. Well, go put your bags away and get out of here. I'll see you back bright and early in the morning."

"Yes, sir. See you in the morning," Bo Jack said and then headed for the door.

He'd almost made it to his bike when footfall sounded behind him.

"Hey, Newbie, where you headed?"

He turned as Skip reached him. "The name's Bo Jack, and I'm heading home."

"You want to go to the soda fountain with us? One of the ladies on Lowell's route waved him over and gave him four dimes. He never hits the milk bottles on her porch in the mornings—hits the step with her paper every time."

Bo Jack glanced over Skip's shoulder at Lowell. The dark-haired boy nodded and walked over, followed by the quieter Dump.

"Yeah, my treat."

Bo Jack stuck his hands in the back pockets of his jeans. "What's the catch?"

"Nothing. We just got started wrong and want to make it right," Lowell said.

Mama didn't expect him at any set time and Clive still had a job for now. "I guess that'd be okay. Thanks. Are they open?"

He couldn't tell them he'd never been to the drugstore soda fountain. They couldn't afford treats at his house.

"Grab your bike and we'll ride over there. They should be open by nine. We can hang out around there 'til then. It's our last week before school starts. We'll have to ride straight to school at the end of our routes then."

Bo Jack rubbed the back of his neck. "Do you boys go to school here in Malvern? I don't remember seeing you."

Skip laughed. "I think Dump here is the only one in the class he started with. Lowell repeated a year and I've repeated more than one 'cause I don't like to go. How about you? We thought you might be new to town."

"I've had a repeat too. We used to live over near the Dixie Curve. You know it?"

"Heard of it. Lots of wrecks and goings-on over there," Skip said.

"I could tell you a few things," Bo Jack said.

They grinned at each other. These guys might just be all right.

Bo Jack ran to his bike and hopped on it.

"How do you ride that crooked thing?" Dump asked.

"Watch me. I'll beat you there."

The other boys ran for their bikes as Bo Jack pedaled to the street. They caught up to him within a block, laughing and grinning.

"Hoot. You sure might, but not without a challenge. Try to keep up," Skip said, passing him.

Bo Jack laughed and stood on his pedals, gained momentum, resumed his seat, and leaned into the rush of speed he'd created. He coasted around corners and jumped curbs all the way to the drugstore.

Ahead of him, Skip and Lowell jumped off their bikes and rushed to the front window. Skip pressed his face to the glass, using his hands to frame his eyes.

"Mr. Pearson is in there. The lights are on in the very back."

Lowell tapped the sign on the front door and slid down to sit against it. "Still an hour before they'll open."

"Maybe," Dump said and disappeared around the corner.

"Where'd he go?" Bo Jack asked.

Skip shrugged and scooted down beside Lowell. "So—what do ya think about football this year?"

Before he could answer, the front door opened, and Lowell tumbled backward.

"Hello, Lowell," Mr. Pearson said, glancing down at the boy at his feet.

Lowell scrambled to his feet. "Good morning, Mr. Pearson."

Dump laughed from behind the man's shoulder. How'd he get into the store?

Skip took his time but pushed off the ground and ambled over to stand beside Bo Jack.

"Dump tells me you boys have delivered all the papers to our fair town this morning. I think that merits a before-hours treat. He tells me Lowell is paying," Mr. Pearson said with a twinkle in his eyes.

Lowell reached in his pocket and produced the change. "Yes, sir."

"In that case, you boys are welcome to come on in, and I'll make you the best ice cream soda you've ever had."

"But, Mr. Pearson, I can only pay for a soda, not any with ice cream."

"Don't you worry none. You pay for the soda and the ice cream part is my treat."

Bo Jack couldn't believe it. He'd never had an ice cream soda.

Mr. Pearson held the door for them to file by. He followed them inside and closed the door. "Grab a stool at the counter."

Bo Jack watched his new friends and followed their lead. The red leather-topped stool moved underneath him. He grabbed onto the edge of the counter and gave it a tentative spin, but grinned and grew still as Mr. Pearson glanced up from scooping ice cream.

"I don't believe I've seen you in here before, son. Who's your father?"

Bo Jack swallowed hard when the eyes of the other boys found him. "Well, sir, my daddy died a long time ago."

The man frowned a bit as if trying to place him. "But is your family from around here?"

"Yes, sir. You probably know my sisters. Maye comes here with James."

The man smiled. "Maye and James. Common enough names, but I do know the ones you're talking about. James just graduated. That young man is going places. He's smart. I have a feeling he intends to marry your sister once she graduates. She's a nice young lady. Neva is also your sister?"

"Yes, sir."

"Now, I know you—you're Bo Jack. You moved from close to the Dixie Curve. I know your brother, Clive and—" He placed the first ice cream soda in front of Bo Jack, garnished with a spoon and straw. "I knew your daddy. A fine man."

Something foreign stirred inside Bo Jack— pride. "Thank you, sir."

The man smiled and continued to make the other three ice cream sodas.

Bo Jack hesitated but decided to try at least a sip. The taste—cold, sweet, creamy—filled his mouth and he closed his eyes and took another sip.

"How is it?"

Bo Jack opened his eyes. Mr. Pearson smiled at him.

"The best one I've ever had."

The man winked at him, and Bo Jack turned his head to find his friends devouring theirs. He joined them.

"Ow—cold, cold," Dump said, grabbing the sides of his temple.

"Slow down, boys. Take your time. You'll still be out of here before we open. Excuse me while I finish a few things," Mr. Pearson said, chuckling and heading to the back of the store.

Bo Jack picked up his spoon. He relished every bite of his and slurped the residual to a noisy finish with his straw. *Man, that was good.*

His friends finished in kind and jumped off their stools.

"Wait. Shouldn't we offer to wash these?" Bo Jack asked.

"Nah," Skip said. "Lowell paid him."

"Still . . . wait a minute," Bo Jack said, sliding off his stool and starting for the back room, but Mr. Pearson emerged and met him before he reached it. "Are you boys finished?"

"Yes, sir. Do you want us to wash up the glasses we used before we go?"

A young man came down the steps from the second level of the store.

"No, Stephen here will take care of it. But thank you for the offer, Bo Jack," Mr. Pearson said.

"You're welcome. Thank you for the treat, sir. Have a good day," he said and jogged to catch up to his new friends who waited by the door.

They left the store and Bo Jack grabbed his bike.

"You some kind of kiss-up or something?" Skip asked.

"No, but right is right."

"I guess."

"Anyway, thanks for including me," Bo Jack said and turned to Lowell. "And thanks for the soda."

Lowell gave him a full smile. "You're welcome. Hey, can I ride along with you? Dump and Skip are headed to the station for some air in their tires. Mine are fine."

"Sure. You want to go swimming?"

"Where?"

"Social Knoll."

"I guess."

"Follow me home, so I can tell Mama or Maye."

"Can I use your phone to call my house?"

"Don't have one."

Lowell's mouth dropped open. "No fooling?"

"Nope, but we could go by your house after mine."

"Okay. Hey, we normally swim in the Ouachita. It's gonna take us a bit to get to Social Knoll on our bikes. I bet my cousin can take us in his car."

"He has a car?"

"Yeah. It's a Model T pickup, but it runs pretty good. My cousin graduates with your sister this year."

"Sounds good to me. Can I leave my bike at your house?"

"Sure. You can put it in the shed with mine."

They made quick stops at their houses. Lowell called his cousin and he came by and picked them up to head to Social Knoll. The place had two swimming holes—a ten-foot hole and a blue hole with clear water, and just past there, on the other side of the hill yet another swimming hole waited. They decided on the ten-foot hole. To Bo Jack's delight, he discovered Billy and Ken swimming there. They swam until mid-afternoon.

Thad, Lowell's cousin, had plans to pick up some friends close to the Dixie Curve for a night out and volunteered to drop Billy and Ken by home. When ready to leave, the bunch of them loaded up into the back of Thad's pickup. They headed out and started up the big steep hill by the ten-foot hole and stalled. The old pickup's bands—the bands that pulled it were worn out—so they got out and Thad tried, but it still wouldn't go.

"Okay, boys, we're going to have to turn this truck around," Thad said.

The group managed to lift and wrestle the lightweight vehicle in the opposite direction.

"Let's try it," Thad ordered.

Thad put it in reverse and they went to pushing until Thad had backed it all the way up that long hill to the top, where they could turn it around and coast down to get back to Malvern. Thad steered to the first gas station on the road. They worked on the bands until they got it going forward again. He dropped Lowell and Bo Jack at Lowell's house.

Kenneth and Billy waved.

"See ya at school," Billy said from the back of the pickup.

Bo Jack waved until they disappeared and then followed Lowell to the shed to get his bike.

"I'll swing by in the morning, and we can ride to the paper together," Lowell said.

"That'll be all right," Bo Jack said, jumping on his bike.

Maybe living in town might turn out fine after all. School could be fun with these new friends. Who knew? He might just settle in here. Clive hadn't left yet. Maybe he wouldn't.

Chapter Sixteen

Visits and Wheels

Clive did leave. At the end of the best school year Bo Jack had ever had, Clive decided the time for California had come. A friend of his had a car and wanted to go out there with him.

Maye graduated and married James. Jake and his other sisters sent money home to help, but uncertainty gripped Bo Jack. He'd begged Maye not to move to Washington DC after her wedding, but she and James both had jobs waiting for them.

The week after Maye left, Mama came in his room after he'd crawled into bed. "How would you like to go on a trip?"

"Where to?"

"Florida."

He scooted into sitting position. "Florida?"

Mama chuckled. "Yes. I thought you'd like that."

"How? Why?"

Mama pulled a letter from her apron pocket. She opened it and handed him a picture.

"That's Neva. Who's that with her?"

"Her husband. Remember she got married, and he has a new job with a propane company in Florida. Your sister is expecting a baby soon. They thought we might want to ride down there with them to their new home and help."

"You bet, Mama. How long will we be there?"

"Well, I'm not sure. Let's just go and see."

"I'd better tell Mr. Jenkins."

"Yes, you need to give him your notice."

"But why?"

"We might be down there all summer. Whenever we get back, you probably should get a job with more pay."

"Yes, ma'am."

Mama smiled and patted his cheek.

"That's my boy." She stood and started toward the door but turned back . "They're coming to pick us up in three weeks. Good night."

"Good night, Mama."

The next morning, Bo Jack dreaded telling his friends and Mr. Jenkins, but they seemed excited for him.

"Just get back here, so we can hear all about it," Skip said.

This made him feel better, but Bo Jack knew he'd miss them.

The swirl of excitement escalated during the trip to Florida. It continued during the first week of setting up his sister's house there, but by the second week in Florida, it fell to dust.

He realized two things: the term *visit* applied to his mother's trip here and the term *move* applied to his. Part of him felt betrayed, but he liked Neva's husband and loved his sister. So if him living in Florida made things easier on Mama, he didn't have a choice.

Mama promised to send for him once she could take care of both of them again. She went home after the birth of his niece.

Bo Jack turned fourteen and attended seventh grade. Being older, he breezed through the year. Neva taught him to drive. Then his brother-in-law helped him get his driver's license and shared a car with him.

Once he had wheels, Bo Jack started enjoying himself more. He bought a pair of sunglasses and a straw hat—too cool.

Bo Jack's only issue came in the form of envy from some of the local boys in the farming area where they lived. First, none of them had cars. Rumors circulated. Someone reported him for racing down the main road of the town doing ninety miles an hour. He hadn't but had to take the school bus to school for a bit. Second, the coach's son's girlfriend, Nora, took a shine to him. This ran him into more trouble.

While riding home from school on the bus one day, another perplexing event happened.

Bo Jack sat in the back talking to his new girlfriend—just talking.

"Boy, I want you to move up front right now," the bus driver said.

"Sir?" Bo Jack asked, glancing up. The man must be joking.

"You heard me. Move away from her."

Nora's smile at the supposed joke fell. All eyes turned back toward them. "We're just talking," she said.

"Don't argue with me. He'll either move or walk home," the driver said.

Anger at this injustice burned inside Bo Jack. He stood and peered down at his girlfriend. "I'll call you later," he said and sauntered to the front of the bus, ignoring the sea of snickers. He met the driver's stern look. "I'll walk."

The man's face reddened, but he pulled over and opened the door. "Fine. Get off my bus."

Bo Jack exited and stood to the side of the road as the bus pulled away. Nora waved at him from the back window. By the time he reached home, gall burned in his stomach. Neva met him at the door, holding his baby niece.

"I was getting worried. Why are you walking?"

He told her.

"Why that's ridiculous. I'm calling the school."

"Don't do that, Neva. I don't want more trouble. Those kids resent me."

She giggled. "If they only knew, little brother. If they only knew." Her laughter always got him. His anger melted and he laughed with her.

But his brother-in-law didn't laugh. He did call the school. Then he put him in another car—this time a blue convertible.

The boys at school took the thrill of driving it away in a moment. They jumped him after school.

Bo Jack tried to keep it in perspective and let it go. He made friends at church in the R.A. boy's group. They collected scrap iron from the local farmers to raise money to go to camp at the start of the summer. He had more fun camping and swimming at the beach with them than he'd had all year. They studied the Bible and his faith grew.

He came home full of hope. Even Nora's parents' opposition to him dating her didn't bother him so much. His mind raced with ideas. Eager anticipation filled him for the rest of the summer.

Until he got the letter from Mama. She had a new beau. They planned to marry, and she wanted him to come home.

"This isn't fair, Neva."

His sister took the letter from him and walked to the kitchen window. She kept her back to him for a minute, and then turned with tears in her eyes. "No, no it's not, but it's probably for the best—for now. You see, we're not sure how much longer we'll be living here anyway. The job situation here isn't stable. We may need to move again. Maybe this will be the last change you have to make until you're through with school. I'm glad Mama's happy."

So that settled it. Bo Jack went back to Mama.

He followed along but didn't mind when things didn't work out the way Mama planned. While sad for her, he didn't get along with the man. Still, he couldn't move back to Florida. Neva wrote them of the continued uncertainty about his brother-in-law's job. So he returned to his old friends.

Skip, Lowell, and Dump acted like he'd never left. Bo Jack got a job with Mr. Pearson's new ice cream shop. It felt good to be home. He did miss having his own wheels though. None of his friends could afford a car either. Except for Bob, another guy they hung out with.

They drove over to the Blue Hole to swim one day in Bob's car and took their dogs. Bob's daddy had bought him a '37 Chevrolet. After a good day of swimming, they headed back on the long gravel road. Lowell elbowed Bo Jack in the back seat.

"Hey, Bob, let me drive," Lowell said.

"No, my daddy wouldn't like that."

"Just for a little bit. I'll go slow."

"No."

Lowell continued to pester Bob until he agreed. Bob pulled over and scooted into the passenger seat. Lowell got out and moved to the front seat. He slid behind the steering wheel and pulled out—slow and careful.

Skip grinned and started rocking back and forth. Bo Jack and Dump grinned and joined him. The back end of that Chevrolet slid on the gravel road. They rocked one way and the whole back end slid over with them, and then they'd go the other way, and it slid to the other side.

"Cut it out, guys," Lowell hollered.

They laughed and the dogs barked.

"Come on, fellas," Bob said.

They quit. Lowell went slow, and the car stopped sliding as they approached the end of the straightaway.

"Watch out, Lowell. There's a curve here," Bob said.

Instead of taking the lower part of the ninety-degree curve, which banked as they went around it, he took the high part where the loose gravel had pushed up to the side—all the way to the edge by a barbed-wire fence. When he did, the car skidded to the side and turned over in the ditch. As they tilted toward the ditch, it flung Dump, Skip, and the dogs against Bo Jack. The car stopped moving. The two dogs barked and licked them.

"Quit kicking me, Bo Jack," Skip hollered.

"I'm not kicking you. You stop kicking me."

"You both stop," Dump said, struggling out of the back-seat pile.

Bo Jack glanced toward the front seat

"Lowell . . . Bob, you all right?"

Silence.

Bob sat there—cool and calm. Lowell kicked the door open and climbed out of the car. Bob reached up and turned the switch key off, shook his head, and crawled out of the car. Bo Jack, Skip, Dump, and the dogs extricated themselves and followed.

By the road, some guys were bailing hay in a field. Lowell caught their attention, and they rushed over. The guys brought their truck and hooked a chain onto the car and pulled it back on its wheels. Bob tried to crank it, but the gas had run out, so Bo Jack hitched back to town and bought twenty cents worth of gas—just a little under a gallon.

Skip put it in, and they managed to make it home. Maybe not having wheels made more sense with these guys. Regardless, it felt good to be home.

Chapter Seventeen

Never Steady and Never Ready

Bo Jack should have known it couldn't last, but he'd hoped. All of his siblings had at least had two constants in their lives—school and friends. Both meant the world to Bo Jack at this point, but Mama struggled. So by the next year, Neva and her husband moved about two hours away, and he went to live with them again. They had a second child now, a son. Things weren't easy for them either, so Bo Jack found a job to help out as much as he could.

He quit trying to fit in at his new school and focused on time with his family. The one unexpected twist came in the form of his teachers there. They made learning interesting— especially his history teacher. Bo Jack excelled in school in ninth grade.

Mama wrote detailed letters to Neva to keep them updated about events back home. Most brought smiles, but the letter they received at the end of February of 1954 brought different tidings.

Bo Jack whistled and unlocked the door.

"Neva, I'm home," he said.

Nothing.

"Where is everybody?"

Bo Jack set his lunchbox on the entry table. The usual exuberant welcome home from his sister didn't come. He started for the kitchen but hadn't taken two steps when Neva appeared. She clutched a letter in her hand and tears streamed down her face.

"I'm so glad your home, baby brother. You need to hear this from me," Neva said, taking his hand and leading him to the couch.

His small niece dashed into the room and reached her arms for him. Bo Jack bent down, but Neva shook her head and picked up her daughter. Neva took his hand, and he shifted to face her. "What is it, Neva? Is it Mama?"

"No, it's Nuben and his wife."

Uncertainty joined the trepidation squeezing the pit of his stomach. "Are they sick? Do we need to go?"

"No." Neva dissolved in tears. He held her hand and took the letter from her unresisting fingers. After a few minutes, Neva scooted back, fishing a handkerchief from her apron pocket. "Read it," she whispered, hugging her daughter to her.

Bo Jack scanned past the first paragraph of greeting and stopped, re-reading the next lines several times: *Nuben and his wife are dead. A train hit the car they were riding in last week.*

Tears filled his eyes and his throat contracted. He looked up in disbelief. Neva shook her head. He peered back at the letter, searching for the how and why.

It seemed they'd been on their way home after an outing with friends. The man driving had dropped off another friend of theirs at his house and had planned to drop Nuben and Patty off next. They never saw the train coming as they drove across the tracks.

"So, they've had the funeral?"

"Yes," Neva said, wiping her nose.

"Poor Aunt Do."

Numbness overcame him; he simply had nothing else to say. Maybe he should write Aunt Do a letter, but what should he say? At least Jimbo had returned from Korea uninjured. Tears spurted again. No, the safe return of one son could not comfort the loss of another. Bo Jack decided to write Mama instead and let her talk to Aunt Do for him.

Memories of his early childhood followed him around the next week. His heart hurt, but nothing could be done. Just like nothing could be done about his brother-in-law's announcement about the ending of his job the next month.

They moved to Houston and Neva delivered her third child by summer's end. Bo Jack found a job with an electric company and liked it. So when Neva came to him to tell him they were moving again, he wanted to stay. His boss even offered to give him a place to live, but his brother-in-law promised to get him a car if he came with them. So he moved with them again and loved his 1936 Ford.

Bo Jack dropped out of school and went to work full-time to help. His brother-in-law made arrangements to trade his car for a 1950 model without telling him.

By the time Christmas of '54 arrived, homesickness gripped his heart. He drove to Arkansas for a few days and then wished he hadn't because leaving again made it worse. Although bittersweet, he enjoyed stopping by to see Aunt Do the most. Even though he loved Mama, she had her agenda and he had his, with both intersecting in the need to survive. So he kissed her good-bye and headed back to Texas.

At least Bo Jack had family to live with. He adored his two nieces and nephew. Neva made a home for him, but his time with them couldn't last. After all, even without a graduation, the time approached for him to go out on his own. This went unsaid, and they settled into a daily rhythm of work, coming home, and starting all over again.

Neva greeted him at the door after work in mid-January of '55. "How was your day?"

Bo Jack took off his sunglasses, put them in his shirt pocket and shoved his keys into his pants pocket. "Fine. Where are the little ones? They always greet me." He laughed, but Neva didn't.

"The baby is sleeping and the other two are out back playing with their father. Bo Jack, I need to talk to you. There's some changes coming." He followed her to the sofa and sat down.

The front door opened, and his brother-in-law burst in the door with the children. They must have run from the back yard to the front to greet him. Squeals of excitement ensued but Neva stood and intercepted her children. "Go play with Daddy. Mommy needs to talk to Uncle Bo Jack."

His brother-in-law scooped up his toddling son and took his daughter by the hand. "Oh, I thought maybe you'd told him already."

Bo Jack's eyes met his sister's, but she shook her head. At least his brother-in-law knew when to push and not to push Neva. He headed for the back of the house.

"Dinner is ready. I'll get it on the table in just a bit," Neva called and then turned back to Bo Jack. A different uncertainty now hung in the air between them.

"What other news, Neva?"

Neva scooted to the edge of the sofa and took both of his hands in hers. "We are moving to California in a month, and this time, you can't come with us. Also, as it is paid for, we need your car."

They couldn't move . . . wait—

"He gave me that car. What am I supposed to do for transportation? I've given you all of my paychecks."

She patted his hands. "Well, that's the thing. All of that stops now. You will keep your checks, and we'll leave the Plymouth. You can finish making the payments on it. It's a '51 and will make you a good car. We'll have the rent here paid through the end of this month. That will give you a couple of weeks to make other living arrangements."

Bo Jack jerked his hands away from her grasp as a flash of temper overcame him. He sprang to his feet and strode to the front window, staring through the tilt of the big venetian blinds. "I need to go for a drive. Don't hold dinner for me," he said.

"Bo Jack, don't leave."

Neva followed him to the door. He ignored her and made a quick exit.

At this point, the loss of his favorite car galled him the most. He'd known the time approached for him to be on his own. But he'd wanted to be the one to announce it. Hm, maybe this worked better as he didn't have to leave them first. They had been good to him. The thought of his nieces and nephew made this preferable. It would have been hard to say he couldn't stay and help anymore.

Bo Jack said a prayer and turned up the radio. Maybe he should go back home this summer and see if he could find work there. If not, a long visit might give him time to decide. His job here covered his current needs, but the town didn't hold enough for him without family.

Life had teetered for him for a long time. How he longed for more, but he'd learned to adapt to whatever life threw at him and make it an adventure. Hopefully, he had a few more good ones.

Chapter Eighteen
Miles To Go

"It's just around this curve," Lowell said.

"Again, who told you about this?" Bo Jack asked, steering around the curve of the remote country road.

"There—the first hill is ahead." Skip pointed out the front window.

The three of them sat in the front seat. Skip rested his elbow on the opened window edge of the passenger door.

Bo Jack slowed a bit, anticipating the first dip Lowell had told him about. His Plymouth went down the first hill and started up the next almost before his back tires could leave the hill behind them. He accelerated to propel them up the next but released as they sped down the other side. This undulating pattern continued through seven identical hills before the road leveled out again.

"Whoop." Lowell slapped Bo Jack on the shoulder from his seat in the middle. "Well navigated, my friend."

"Turn around," Skip said. "Let's do it again."

Bo Jack's heart raced. They did have to retrace their journey to go home. He found a dirt road and used it to turn around and head toward home. "Here we go again, boys," he said, laughing.

Bo Jack navigated six of the hills with deft precision. His stomach caught up with the rest of his body on the way up the seventh hill. Just as he topped its summit, they met a little Ford coupe, coming up the hill. Instead of staying to one side, the driver met them straight in the middle of the road. Bo Jack tried to navigate as best he could, but when he tapped his brakes to slow down, the back end of his car had a mind of its own.

Skip dove for the back seat just as the coupe slammed into their fender. The car careened off the ground and pulled toward the four-foot ditch next to them. They flipped before Skip could reach the back seat.

Weeds scraped each side of Bo Jack's car as they passed through a ditch, slid down a hill and out into the woods in his upside-down car. Skip and Lowell landed on the headliner.

"Quit kicking me," Skip yelled.

"I ain't kicking you," Lowell said.

Memories of their previous wreck in Bob's car came to Bo Jack's mind. He gripped the steering wheel to keep from falling into his friends. Dust billowed through the open window. He didn't think they'd ever stop, but a few seconds later, they did when the windshield toppled to the ground in front of the front bumper.

Bo Jack tried to get his horn to stop blowing, but it wouldn't, so he turned the key off and fell down onto the headliner with Skip and Lowell, skinning his shin in the process. "Ouch. You guys hurt?"

"No, except for a few bruises from Lowell kicking me," Skip said.

"I didn't kick you."

Bo Jack winced and climbed out of the open window. Skip and Lowell scrambled out behind him. They dusted off their pants and scurried up toward the wrecked Ford coupe. It appeared the car had gone sideways and the driver had jumped the ditch behind them before continuing toward the wooded area, but had stopped before they did.

Lowell ran toward the car. Bo Jack and Skip followed.

An old woman sat in the front seat, moaning. Lowell hesitated and looked back at them.

Bo Jack hobbled over to her window. "Are you hurt, ma'am?"

She nodded and squinted at him. "My ribs are hurting. Do I know you, young man?"

Bo Jack opened her car door and helped her out. "No, ma'am. I don't think so." Bo Jack turned to his buddies. "Can you guys run to that farm we passed and call an ambulance?"

"If they have a phone," Lowell said.

Skip took off with Lowell on his heels.

The lady gripped Bo Jack's arm as he hobbled toward the back of the car.

"I think we should wait here," she said, leaning against the trunk.

"Let me check something first," Bo Jack said.

He checked for leaking gas but couldn't find any, so he returned to stand with her.

"You look a bit familiar, young man. What is your name?"

Bo Jack told her, which brought a smile.

"I knew your daddy. In fact, I grew up with both of your parents."

"I'm sure sorry about this wreck, ma'am."

"What? It was my fault, not yours. I didn't even think about meeting someone at this time of day and hogged the road. You tried to go to the side, but there isn't one here—only that ditch. No, this is my fault."

"Still, I'm sorry we came at this time of day and you got hurt."

The lady gave him a sweet smile. "You are nice. Just like your daddy."

Lowell and Skip came running back. "The farmer saw what happened and called an ambulance. It should be here soon," Lowell said.

Skip hung back, but Bo Jack introduced both of them.

The ambulance lights appeared. Two men jumped out and ran over to them. The sheriff arrived. He talked to the lady first and then the boys. The sheriff went to inspect their vehicles and came back.

"Well, boys. She says she was in the middle of the road, so you're not getting arrested or in trouble. But your car is totaled, so I'll have to give you a ride back to town. I'll call and have them tow the cars to the yard."

Bo Jack shot his friends a look. He hadn't even finished making the car payments.

They slid into the back of the sheriff's car.

"Do you still have your bike?" Skip whispered.

Bo Jack rolled his eyes. "No, I sold it to Mr. Pearson for a three-cent nickel."

"Then you're flat out of luck," Lowell said, snickering.

The sheriff got into the car.

Bo Jack bit his lip and stared out the window all the way back to town. The sheriff dropped him off first.

Mama met him at the door.

"I'm okay, but my car isn't."

"What happened?"

He gave her the short version.

"Is your leg bleeding?"

Mama hated blood. Bo Jack smiled. "Just a little. The men from the ambulance checked it. I'm fine, Mama."

"Sit down and I can chip off some ice for you to put on it." Bo Jack sat at the table.

"Son, you can't keep running around with Skip and Lowell like that. You need to think about your future. I had hopes when you arrived here and hired on at the dairy, but ever since summer started, the three of you are acting like kids instead of young men. You'll be eighteen next month."

"I'm working hard for the dairy in the mornings, making deliveries in their trucks. I'm upset about my car, Mama, but I can't get another one right now. I'll just have to leave earlier to walk there. You walk everywhere."

Mama handed him an ice-filled cloth. He rolled up the leg of his jeans. A mixture of dried and fresh blood covered the skinned area. Bruises formed, so he placed the rag on them, wincing.

"Don't get smart with me. You know I'm right. Unless you hope to run the dairy one day, there is no future there. Another teenaged boy can take your place next week."

"Gee thanks, Mama." She sat in the chair next to his and scooted it to face him. "I heard you've taken Suzie out a few times since you got home. Are you hoping to settle down here?"

"Mama, I've only been home a few months."

"You need to be thinking about things."

Bo Jack rolled down his pant leg and hobbled over to the sink. He emptied the chipped ice from the cloth, rinsed the blood from it, and squeezed it before draping it on the edge of the sink to dry. "I am, Mama." He dropped a kiss on the top of her head. "I'm heading to bed."

The next day, after morning milk deliveries, he went to the hospital to check on the lady who'd hit them. Lowell met him there, but Skip didn't come. It felt awkward, but Bo Jack could tell she appreciated their visit.

They went to Lowell's house afterward, and Bo Jack called Suzie. "Hey, I wanted to call and apologize. I can't pick you up for our date tonight. We got in a wreck last night—yeah, but anyway, I'm at Lowell's and we're heading to the mill pond by you to fish. You want to come?"

Bo Jack placed the receiver back in the cradle and glanced at Lowell. "She doesn't want to fish, but said if we want to stop by, her daddy left a jar of White Lightning. He told her to pour it out, but as we're coming by, she'll save it for us."

"You ever drank any?"

"No. Have you?"

"No."

A grin crept across Lowell's face, then spread to Bo Jack's. They grabbed their fishing gear and headed out on foot.

Suzie opened the door before Bo Jack could knock and held her finger to her lips. She sure looked pretty. He smiled at her. They followed her to the woodpile. She slid a jar from behind it and handed it to Bo Jack. He propped their fishing gear against the pile and took the jar.

"There you go," she said.

"We can't drink it here," he said.

"Let's go to the railroad trestle," Lowell suggested.

Bo Jack took Suzie's hand. Her dog ran toward them from the road and followed them to the trestle bridge.

Lowell studied the jar of clear liquid and said, "I tell you what—I'll back you out—you drink half of it and I'll drink the other half."

Bo Jack glanced at Suzie and she giggled. He grimaced. "Man, I don't know."

"I double dog dare ya."

Bo Jack handed him the jar. "Well, here, you drink your half first."

Lowell drank half of it, coughed and sputtered, and handed the jar to Bo Jack. He sniffed it and

Suzie laughed. Taking a deep breath, he downed it. By this time, the effects had hit Lowell.

"Look at him," Suzie said.

Lowell chased Suzie's dog and dove but missed it, then laughed as he landed on the rocks near the tracks. The dog ran farther away and Lowell chased him. Suzie and Bo Jack followed.

"Don't you hurt my dog, Lowell," Suzie said. Lowell dove and missed again.

Bo Jack's vision blurred, and he shook his head but kept walking. It cleared and he reached down to help Lowell to his feet. The world tilted and Bo Jack stumbled.

Suzie laughed. "Oh, dear. You can't let Daddy see you. He will know I gave you the jar."

They continued toward her house. A car slowed behind them, so they moved to the side, but the car stopped instead of passing them. The driver rolled the windows down and hollered at him.

"Hey, Dump."

Lowell jogged back to them. Dump jumped out of the car. "What have you boys been drinking?"

"White Lightning," Bo Jack said, stumbling forward.

"Whoa, hold up—I'd better drive you two back to town."

Bo Jack looked back at Suzie and started to turn, but Dump opened the car door and guided him inside. "I'll see Suzie to her door."

"She's my girl, Dump."

"Yes, I am," she giggled.

The world tilted again. Bo Jack's stomach didn't feel so good. Dump climbed back in the car and headed toward town. "You want me to drop you by your house, Bo Jack?"

"No. Mama will see your car and come to check on us. She'll know we've been drinking and that Lowell's drunk."

Lowell half-moaned and half-laughed. "Just me?" Dump laughed outright.

Bo Jack's head didn't feel right. He made out the sign by his street. "Just drop us here. I need to put up my rod and reel." He'd worked to buy it, a little each week, from his paper route. Mama had said he should buy something just for him for his hard work. She had stored it safe for him while he'd been gone.

"What about Lowell's?" Dump asked.

"Give it to me."

Dump pulled over and helped them from the car. Bo Jack teetered when he handed him their fishing gear.

"Are you sure?"

Bo Jack took a deep breath. "Sure." Lowell leaned against the car.

Dump eyed him and laughed. "Can you walk?" Lowell nodded and ambled forward. Dump shook his head and went around to the driver's side, got in, and pulled away with a final wave.

"You wait here, Lowell. I'm going to try to slide these in the kitchen."

"I'll go with ya."

"No. If Mama sees you, she'll know we've been drinking." Bo Jack assessed his unsteady friend. "Come on, but you ain't going inside."

They made it to the small side porch by the kitchen. Bo Jack crouched down and crawled up the steps with their fishing gear, reached up to turn the knob, and cracked it open. It looked like Mama must be in the back, so he slid the rods inside, shut the door, and back-crawled down the steps.

"Lowell?" His friend sat on the bottom step with his eyes half-opened. "Is anyone at your house?"

"Mama's or Daddy's?"

Oh yeah, he remembered Lowell's parents had divorced a couple of years before. "Your Mama's—it's closer."

Lowell pursed his lips. "Nope, no one's home. Let's go." But he didn't move.

Bo Jack helped Lowell up and they staggered toward the neighbor's back yard. They made it all the way to Mrs. Yance's clothesline. Lowell grabbed onto it and the clothes shook. Bo Jack pulled him away, and they staggered toward the fence in the next yard. They attempted to climb the fence but didn't clear it and fell back into his neighbor's yard. Lowell stumbled into the clothesline again, tearing it down and scattering the clothes on the ground. Bo Jack freed him from the line. He decided they'd better go around the yard.

They finally made it to Lowell's mother's house—she lived nearby, but his dad lived across town. They sat on the porch for the longest and dozed a bit.

Bo Jack woke up sweating. His stomach felt terrible. He reached in his pocket and found a few coins and stood. "Lowell, wake up. I'm going to the movie. It's cooler and dark in there."

Lowell lifted his head when Bo Jack stumbled off the porch. "No. You can't go. You're drunk."

Bo Jack ignored him and staggered toward Main Street. He reached the corner and turned toward the theater.

"Catch him. Somebody catch him." What? He turned back and Lowell trailed along behind him hollering.

Bo Jack waved him off and continued on his way until Skip came walking toward him with his arms spread wide, trying to catch him. Bo Jack laughed and grabbed hold of the parking meter next to him to keep from falling. Then he ran out into the middle of Main Street and back toward Lowell. Skip ran up and grabbed him, guiding him back toward the sidewalk. Lowell caught up to them.

"What gives? I see you boys have been having fun without me. Where'd you get the liquor?"

Bo Jack mumbled their tale.

Skip laughed and punched his shoulder. "Take me next time." He threw one arm around Lowell's shoulder and one arm around Bo Jack's. "Hey, do you guys have any money?"

Lowell opened one eye and met Bo Jack's bleary gaze. They disentangled themselves, neither so much under the influence as to give Skip money. They knew better.

"Nah, I'm tapped out," Lowell said.

Bo Jack shook his head and wished he hadn't. He grabbed another parking meter.

"Well, I got to go. You boys clear your heads," Skip said.

"See ya," Bo Jack said.

"I don't feel so good," Lowell moaned.

Bo Jack abandoned the movie idea and grabbed his friend's arm. They made it back to Lowell's mother house and sat in the backyard until about ten o'clock that night. No one came home and no one checked on them.

"I got to go home. Man, I can't take this anymore," Bo Jack said.

"Well, you go on. You go—"

"I ain't gonna leave you here like this—sitting by the back door. I'll walk you home. See you get to your dad's and then go home."

"No, you go, you go."

Bo Jack hesitated, but decided he'd best get home.

The night air cleared his head as he walked, but his mouth felt like cotton. Bo Jack crept into the dark house and could hear Mama snoring in her room. He tiptoed to the bathroom and then to his room. He fell face down on his bed and didn't know anything more until morning.

"Bo Jack, wake up. It's time for church." He moaned and pushed up in his bed.

"Mama, I'm not feeling very good."

She walked into the room putting on her hat. "What's the matter?"

"I stayed over at Lowell's too late."

Mama pulled on her gloves. She leaned over him and made a face. "Hmph—you need church from what I smell, but I guess you'd better stay home. You're about grown, but I don't want any more of this. Do you understand?"

"Yes, ma'am. I don't want any more of it either," he said holding his pounding head.

"Good."

Mama spun around, and the door closed a few minutes later.

Bo Jack threw back the covers and made for the bathroom. His stomach rolled so he hung over the toilet for a suspended eternity. Afterwards, he splashed his face and brushed his teeth. After throwing on some clothes, he headed to Lowell's mother's house. He knocked on the door, but no one answered. Maybe Lowell had made it back to his dad's.

Bo Jack circled to the backyard to check. No one by the back door, but something sounded in the garage and he headed there. Lowell's mother kept an old Essex that didn't run. Moaning emanated from the car. Bo Jack found Lowell sitting in the backseat.

"Good morning," Bo Jack said, grinning.

Lowell moaned again and opened the door. He crawled out and leaned against the back of the car. "No, it ain't and don't you ever share no drink with me again."

Bo Jack laughed and held out his hand. "Deal."

Lowell shook his hand. "Deal. I got to get home to my dad's. I'll bet I'm in big trouble. Mother doesn't even know I spent the night out here. She parked out front last night and left for church earlier. I didn't want her to know."

"Come on. I'll walk with ya," Bo Jack said. "Do you think he has coffee?"

"Yeah."

Bo Jack's sobering mind pondered many things as they walked. "Lowell, do you want to stay here for the rest of your life?"

Lowell shrugged.

"I kind of thought I did, but I'm not so sure. You're gonna graduate this year. I'm not. I've got to find another plan."

Lowell stopped. "You leaving again?"

Bo Jack couldn't say anything for a bit and picked up his pace. Lowell caught up with him. They walked in silence for the next couple of blocks.

"Maybe I should try California. Lots of people are finding jobs out there—Neva's family, Clive, and some of our other friends. I'm not helping Mama that much. She loves me but is asking me if I have plans to get married."

"What about Suzie?"

"I can't provide for her, Lowell. Shoot, I need to see if I can provide for myself."

Lowell wiped his forehead with the back of his hand. "Maybe we can table this for another day."

Bo Jack laughed. "Sure. Let's get you home."

Chapter Nineteen

Maps, Craps, and Time Snaps

"How much do you have, Bo Jack?"

"Ninety-five dollars."

"Gene?"

The third guy sitting in Dump's '52 Dodge opened an empty wallet and turned out empty pockets. "Zilch, but please let me go. I'll pay you guys back once we get out there. I need a job. If there's no job in Hammond, Indiana, we can go to California. My brother lives in Torrance."

"I've got forty-five bucks," Dump said.

"We may be crazy, but we're going," Bo Jack said.

They'd all said their goodbyes and loaded up early that morning.

Bo Jack had decided Mama might be right about his job at the dairy. Still, of the three of them, he was the only one working. Even though Dump had graduated, he hadn't found a job all summer. Jimbo had sent his friend, Gene, to them. Bo Jack had promised they'd give him a ride, so money or zilch, Gene was going.

"Good to know," Dump said and pulled away from Gene's parents' house.

They headed north. Bo Jack kept the map unfolded on his lap.

A few hours into the trip, as they cruised through another little town, a loud pop followed by a rotating thud, thud, thud came from the right front of the car. Dump steered to the side of the road. "You guys stay here with the car, and I'll go get us a tire at that station up ahead," Dump said.

"You don't have a spare?" Gene asked.

"Nope. I'd hoped these tires would hold out until I could get work, but I guess not."

"We'll get the tire off while you're gone," Bo Jack said.

Twenty minutes later, Dump returned with the tire.

"How much did it cost?"

"Twenty-five. Now I'm down to twenty."

"I'll buy the bologna and bread for lunch," Bo Jack said with a grin.

"Thanks. Help me with this tire." They made quick work of it and got back on the road, stopping at a little market on the edge of town for a few groceries.

Bo Jack consulted the map and navigated them to St. Louis. Soot-stained buildings greeted them.

"What a dreary city," Gene said.

"You can say that again," Bo Jack said.

"Let's stop and get a little gas," Dump suggested.

They stopped and Dump rolled down the window. The gas attendant hurried over.

"Fill her up."

"Yes, sir."

"Hey, ask him about that black soot on the buildings," Bo Jack said.

The attendant came back to collect payment and Dump paid him. "What's the deal with the black stuff on the buildings?"

"That's from years of burning coal here."

"Oh, we didn't know."

"Yes, sir, you'll see some more of it as you travel north. Where are you headed?"

"Indiana."

"Yep, you'll see some more."

"Thanks."

Dump steered onto the road but slowed after a few miles. "I don't know about you guys, but I don't want to work in a dreary town. If Indiana is like St. Louis, I think California might be better."

Bo Jack opened the car pocket and pulled out a couple of other maps. "Let's go."

"I'm in, guys," Gene said from the backseat.

They turned around and headed toward Joplin and drove all the way to downtown Tulsa before they stopped at a hotel for the night. Early the next morning, they hit the road again. Bo Jack used a pencil to navigate their route down through Oklahoma City to Amarillo, Texas, and on to Roswell, New Mexico.

Mama had told him Mary and her husband had moved there, so he stopped at a pay phone to call her for directions to her house, then climbed back in the car.

"Are you going to ask her for some money?" Dump asked.

"We'll just have to see. I haven't seen her in years, and I don't know how they're doing. If it doesn't seem right, I won't. I want to see her though."

Mary stood by her driveway, no longer the teenaged girl he remembered. Still pretty as ever, but older. Bo Jack didn't realize how much he'd missed her until he saw her.

Dump turned into the driveway and Bo Jack jumped out and ran around the front of the car. He stopped a few feet short of hugging her. Awkwardness gripped him.

Mary smiled up at him. "Look at you, Bo Jack. Your hair's darkened like the rest of us. My, you're full grown and tall like our daddy."

"Yes, ma'am. How are you, Mary?"

She looked back toward the house and then at the car. "I'm fine. My son—your nephew—is taking a nap, so I can't invite you in right now. My daughter is at school."

Bo Jack stuffed his hands in his back pockets. He couldn't ask her for money.

"I'd love to meet them, but we have to keep going. I just wanted to stop by and see you."

Mary's eyes glistened, and she bridged the distance between them to reach up and hug him. Bo Jack pulled his hands out of his pockets and hugged her back. What had happened to Mary? There was a sadness about her, but he knew he couldn't ask.

She pulled back, smoothed his collar, and patted his shoulder. "You be careful and call Clive once you get out there. Do You have his address and number?"

"I do," Bo Jack said, glancing back at the car.

Dump inclined his head toward the passenger seat.

Bo Jack turned back to Mary. She smiled. "I know. You've got to go. I love you, little brother."

"Love you, Mary. Now that I have your address, I'll send you a post card."

"You do that."

Bo Jack gave her another quick hug, breathing in the vestige of home and family. He released her and hurried back to the car.

Dump backed out and Bo Jack gave one last wave. "What's Mary doing living here? I thought she went to New York when she left home," Dump said.

Bo Jack stared at him. "I didn't know you knew Mary."

"I don't, but my cousin graduated with her."

"Yes, she lived in New York. She's married and has children. I've got so many nieces and nephews between Aggy, Neva, and Mary. Jake and his wife adopted a baby. They brought him by Neva's one time while I was staying with them. We didn't get to visit long."

"With the way jobs are nowadays, no one has time for long visits. I'm ready to see my brother," Gene said.

"We've got to get to California first," Dump said. "Direct me, Bo Jack."

He pulled out the map and directed them to the right road. They limited stops and drove on to

Stratford, Arizona, and then coasted fourteen or fifteen miles into Globe, Arizona—almost out of gas. Once they bought some, they continued on to Phoenix.

"I need to sleep," Dump said as they left the city. He pulled over to the side of the road.

"I can drive," Bo Jack said.

"No, let's all get some shut-eye and drive on to California tomorrow."

Bo Jack turned on his side and used his arm to pillow his head against the window. He shut his eyes, but the sound of passing cars kept him awake. Dump snored, and Gene's breaths sounded long and even from the backseat.

He stared at the twinkling stars in the inky sky. Would Clive let him stay with him? His eyelids became heavy and closed.

The sound of the engine starting woke Bo Jack. He opened his eyes. A few stars glistened in the light of dawn. He turned his head to find Dump behind the wheel. "It's close to sunrise. I'm ready to get there," Dump said.

Bo Jack yawned and straightened in his seat. He rolled down the window and breathed in the fresh air. "Let's go then. I don't mind driving, though."

"Nah, I'll drive."

Gene stirred about an hour later.

By the time they reached Los Angeles, Bo Jack had five dollars and the other two had nothing. They dropped Gene by his brother's house in Torrance after stopping to ask for directions. Gene's brother gave them a map of Los Angles so they could find their way to Clive's house.

They rounded the corner to find a small wood-framed house fronted by a porch with a wrought-iron banister. The porch light glowed by the door. No one answered when he knocked. Bo Jack turned to leave, but the door opened.

"May I help you? Wait, are you looking for Clive?"

"Yes, sir. I'm his brother."

"I can see the resemblance," the old man said. "He lives here. Rents the room in back. He's at work at his second job—he works as a night watchman. I'll give you directions to get there."

"Thank you." Bo Jack returned to the car and directed Dump to Clive's work. A man at the gate told them to wait there.

Clive appeared a few minutes later. His serious expression gave way to a slow smile.

"What are you doing out here, boy?"

Bo Jack glanced at the man behind his brother and decided against hugging Clive. He stuck out his hand. His brother shook it with a knowing lift of his eyebrow.

"I rode out with two guys."

Clive glanced back at Dump in the car by the gate and waved.

"I recognize Dump. Where's the other fella?"

"We dropped him off at his brother's place in Torrance. He's Jimbo's friend."

"What's his name?"

"Gene—"

"Gene. You boys do grow up. I've run into his brother a couple of times since I came. He's hooked up with one of the labor unions. Speaking of that, have you looked for work yet?"

"No, sir. We just got here."

"How much money you got?"

Bo Jack peered down at the ground. "I had the most when we first left, but we rolled in on my last five." Clive didn't laugh. He reached into his back pocket for his wallet.

"I got twenty dollars here. You take it."

Bo Jack waved his hands in front of him. "No, we'll make our way, Clive. I just wanted you to know I was here."

Clive held up the twenty. "Listen to me, boy. I'm going to give you the name of a place where you can rent a room and eat cheap. This will start you off, but the rest is up to you. Take it."

Bo Jack met his brother's steady gaze and nodded. He took the money and reached for his own wallet. "Thank you, Clive. I really appreciate it."

Clive reached over and grasped his shoulder. "This is my second job. My main job is working as a carpenter. I promised Daddy to see you kids grown. You take it from here. Let me know once you find work. I might be able to help you get some wheels—can't promise though. A guy is behind in his payments to me on a car. If he doesn't catch up this week, I'll take it back. But don't count on it."

Bo Jack nodded and swallowed the lump in his throat. Seeing Clive here made him realize what his brother had sacrificed for them. "Thank you—for everything. You've done more for me than I can ever repay."

Clive turned his head and cleared his throat. He took a cigarette and a book of matches out of his pocket. "I might as well have a smoke since I had to take my break to see you," he said, striking a match. He lit the end of the cigarette and shook out the match.

"Sorry 'bout that. Your landlord said it'd wouldn't be a problem," Bo Jack said.

Clive blew out smoke. "It's not, but you two need to get out of here and get a room. Start looking for work early in the morning. Come on and I'll give Dump directions."

Bo Jack followed his brother to where Dump waited. He patted Clive on the shoulder and slid in the car. Clive stood by Dump's window and told him how to get to the rooming place. Once he finished, he backed away.

Bo Jack leaned forward. "I'll let you know how we come out with everything. Thanks again."

Clive nodded, threw his cigarette down, and ground out the end with the sole of his shoe. He waved and headed back toward the gate.

Clive's money bought them a room for a week and the rest of Bo Jack's money bought them a bowl of chili with beans at a little place close to where they stayed. It took them close to a week to find work. They took the first job offers they received—construction for three dollars twenty-five cents an hour. Bo Jack didn't mind it, but Dump didn't like it.

"I got a high school education, and I ain't digging a ditch for nobody," Dump said.

They stuck with it and earned a twenty-five cent raise by the end of the first month. It kept them in their room, fed them, and paid for gas. Clive couldn't get him the car he'd told him about because the man caught up on his payments. So Bo Jack had to rely on Dump for his transportation, and Dump still wanted to quit at the start of the second month even though their boss promised to give them another small raise.

"I called Gene at his brother's house. He wants us to meet them in Long Beach tomorrow at a labor-union meeting. He says we can get better jobs working with the union," Dump said.

"I'm with you," Bo Jack said.

At the meeting, the men speaking made it sound good. The boys joined and received the address of an oil company to report to for jobs the next day. Bo Jack wasn't convinced of the benefit but agreed to it for Dump's sake. Gene and his brother took them to the local fair afterward. They took a couple of silly pictures and headed back to Los Angeles.

By the next day, they had new jobs making seven fifty an hour, but instead of building things, they dug ditches in more than 115-degree heat. They took salt tablets to make them sweat enough to stay cool. The supervisors made the men work fifteen minutes and stand in the shade fifteen minutes for the whole day. Soon, they moved Bo Jack to running a jackhammer for more money, but once they completed the job at that site, the job ended.

Next, they sent them to the docks to unload coffee beans, but the foreman refused to hire Bo Jack without a birth certificate to prove his age. He'd never thought to get a copy of his, so he sat in the car every day while Dump worked that week. Then they had to wait a week for Dump to get paid.

Once Dump had his money, Bo jack challenged him to a dice game and took his whole check. He offered to give it back, but Dump refused. Bo Jack used it for them both anyway.

After another week, Bo Jack still couldn't find another job and Dump had had enough.

"This isn't what I expected. I can find something like this or better closer to home."

Bo Jack flopped on his bed. "We don't have enough money to go home right now. Come on, we should stick with it a little longer. I wrote Mama and she can have them send me a copy of my birth certificate."

"Hold off on that. Let's go get something to eat, and I don't mean chili and beans. Let's go to that burger joint on the corner. I'm buying."

The smell hit them before they even reached the corner. "That reminds me of that place by the old five-and-dime at home," Dump said.

"It does. I can remember smelling it when I rode my bicycle by it. I never had enough to stop, but it sure smelled good."

"Well, we're eating burgers tonight." They opened the door to find the place half-filled. The waitress walked by them, holding a tray.

"Grab a booth. I'll be back to take your order," she said.

They slid into the nearest empty booth.

The waitress returned and took out her order pad. "What'll it be?"

"Two burgers and two cokes," Dump said.

Bo Jack nodded, and she disappeared.

Dump sat across from him, facing in the direction of the door. Bo Jack could hear the bell jangle above the door several times but couldn't see who walked in the place. Someone put money in the jukebox. Bo Jack drummed in time on the tabletop until the waitress slid his plate in front of him. He waited for Dump to get his before taking his first bite.

"This is the best burger I've ever had. I—"

"Look who just walked in here," Dump said, placing his burger back on the plate.

Bo Jack turned, and a grin spread across his face.

A boy—now a young man—they knew from school walked over to them.

"Walter, what are you doing out here?" Dump said, standing up to shake their friend's hand.

Walter shook it but waved Bo Jack down. "Keep your seat, keep your seat. I'll slide in with ya." Bo Jack moved his plate and drink over, making room for Walter.

The waitress hurried over and took Walter's order before he could answer Dump's question. After she sped away, he turned back to them. "I'm working for one of the big motor companies here, but I'm about ready to go back home. How about you fellas?"

Bo Jack glanced at Dump and laughed. "It's funny you said that. We've been here a couple of months but are about ready to head home ourselves. Lack of cash is the only thing keeping us here."

Walter glanced from Dump to Bo Jack. He grinned. "Do either of you have a car?"

"I do," Dump said.

"Then we're set. I've got money to get home, but no transportation. Together, we can all go."

The waitress returned with Walter's food.

Bo Jack couldn't believe it. Part of him wanted to stay and see if he could find a better job, but he couldn't do it without a car.

Walter had to give a week's notice at his job, so they planned to leave at the end of the next week. Bo Jack wrote to Mama and called Clive.

So much for the West Coast—time moved them forward and time moved them back. This achieved nothing for him. He'd have to head out again once he returned home. The uncertainty of the where and how bothered him, but he'd just have to wait and see.

Chapter Twenty

Climbing Trees and a Red Dress

The familiar sound of the train greeted them as they crossed the bridge into town.

"We made it, boys," Walter said, leaning over the back seat smiling. Dump exhaled and rubbed his face with one hand and kept steering with the other.

For once, Bo Jack didn't say anything. This time, coming home felt different. He stared out the window at the intersection where'd he'd wrecked his bicycle. The train whistle sounded again. Bo Jack closed his eyes and thought about Nuben, hobos and hams, and Aunt Do. He needed to go see her.

Dump veered to the right at the fork, turned on Bo Jack's street, and stopped in front of his house. "Here you go," he said. "Come by when you decide what you're going to do."

Bo Jack nodded and opened the door. A cold gust of the January wind hit his face. He shivered, jumped out, and slammed the door.

Walter climbed out of the back. "Brr, we're not in California anymore." He handed Bo Jack his suitcase.

"Thanks."

"Take care, Bo Jack."

He turned toward the house and found Mama standing on the landing outside the kitchen door. She smiled, he smiled back and strode across the yard to her. "Good morning, Mama."

"Good morning. Get on in here," she said, giving him a hug.

They went inside and he took his suitcase to the back room. She followed him. "I've got news for you. I know you've been in and out the last few years, but do you remember Madge and Robert next door?"

"Where BJ lives? He's younger than me. I remember when they bought the house. Why?"

"Well, BJ is Madge's younger brother. She has another brother you've never met, but I have. He came back from Korea and worked for the same company he had before he left. He's a crew boss for a tree company. Anyway, I was telling her about you returning home and needing a job. She talked to Harley on the phone last night. It turns out one of his men has transferred to Dallas, and he's in need of another man on the crew he's running in Longview, Texas, right now."

"Longview, Texas? A tree company?"

"The company is not out of there. According to Madge, it's just where one of their contracts is right now. I'm not sure about all of it, but anyway, he has some work for you. He said you could catch a bus and come to Longview, or if you wanted to wait, he's coming here this weekend to see family and you can ride back with him—if you're interested."

"I'll wait for him to come home this weekend and talk to him."

She stared up at him for a moment and beamed. "My goodness, you've grown up, haven't you?"

His stomach growled loud enough for Mama to hear it. She laughed and turned toward the hallway. "I'll get you some coffee and something to eat. I want to hear about Mary and Clive. Tell me how they looked and about California."

Bo Jack followed her to the kitchen. He pulled out a chair and sat down at the table.

"Mary seemed sad to me," he said.

Mama held the egg above the pan for a minute. "Did she?" She cracked the egg on the side and released it into the frying pan. It sizzled.

"Yes, and I didn't get to see my niece and nephew. Has she written to you?"

Mama flicked some grease over the egg, flipped it once, and turned off the burner. She grabbed a plate, slid the egg onto to it, and brought it, along with a plate of toast, to him. "Last month."

He searched her face. "What am I missing?"

She gave his shoulder a playful push and smiled. "Nothing, son. Your sister had some challenging times when she first left home, but she's married now. I just wanted to hear about her and my grandchildren. Let me get the toast I made earlier and some coffee."

"She looked good, and Clive is doing fine. Have you heard from Neva? I've missed them."

"Yes, in fact, I had a letter yesterday." She brought two steaming cups on saucers to the table and slid into the chair opposite of him. "I'll let you read it, but I want to know about California."

He tipped his cup, pouring coffee into the saucer to cool. "Let me tell you about the ocean."

They talked for over two hours. It might have been one of the best conversations he'd had with her. She laughed more than he'd ever heard her laugh.

She glanced up at the kitchen clock. "Look at the time. I'd better run next door and tell Madge. Harley is supposed to call again tomorrow. She can tell him your plans then."

"I said I'd talk to him, Mama," he said, but she grabbed her coat and dashed out the door.

Bo Jack shook his head and took their dishes to the sink, washed them, and set them to dry on the drainer rack. He wiped his hands on the dish towel and draped it to the side of the rack. Out the kitchen window, stood the lone tree in the front yard. Those work crews he'd seen clearing downed trees or tending big ones in people's yards came to mind. Would that be what he'd be doing? Well, he'd just have to wait and talk to the man. Right now—a yawn stopped him—he wanted a nap. He hoped Mama didn't mind.

Bo Jack headed to the back bedroom of the two-bedroom house. The absence of his siblings didn't make it feel bigger, just quieter. He fell across one of the small twin beds and slept.

He didn't wake up again until almost suppertime when the delicious aroma of Mama's cooking woke him. Skip turned up at the door just as Mama put their plates on the table. Bo Jack invited him inside.

"Hey, I heard you were back. You want to grab a movie?"

Bo Jack glanced back at the table. "We're just sitting down to supper."

"Have you eaten, Skip?" Mama asked.

"No, ma'am."

"Sit down then. You join us and then the two of you can go to town."

Skip grinned and Bo Jack shook his head. Some things never changed. His friend loved to eat, and a free meal always agreed with him.

"I haven't seen you in town much since Bo Jack left, Skip. What have you been up to?" Mama said placing another plate on the table.

Skip shrugged. "Oh, this and that. My friends ran out on me to make their way in this world, but they ended up back here. At least Lowell is still here and now Bo Jack is back. So why should I leave?"

"I may not be here long. Mama says our neighbor's brother has an opening on his crew in Texas," Bo Jack said.

Skip took the bowl of potatoes Mama passed him and spooned some on his plate. He laughed. "Man oh man, here we go again."

Bo Jack couldn't help smiling. He took the bowl from his friend. They finished filling their plates. The smell of Mama's cooking may have woken him, but the taste completed his homecoming. "Mama, this is the best meal I've had in forever."

She smiled and sighed. "It's good to have you home."

They cleaned their plates and left for the picture show downtown. He told Skip about his travels and jobs. Skip had managed to find a few odd jobs here and there. He wanted to stay close to home.

After the show let out, they hurried back to Mama's. Bo Jack sniffed and coughed in the cold air. "Do you know anyone who could drive me out to see Aunt Do for a little bit tomorrow? I'm kind of stuck, but I'd like to see her."

"No, I don't. Maybe you can write her a letter. Does your Mama ever get out to see her or does she come to town?"

"Not often," Bo Jack said. "Now tell me, do you have a girlfriend?"

Skip grinned and bumped him with his shoulder. "If you stay in town, you can meet her. How about you? Did you fall in love in California?"

They stopped at the corner and let the traffic pass before crossing.

"Are you kidding? We were too broke to do much of anything, but there were some pretty ones out there."

They crossed Main Street and chatted the rest of the way home.

"Well, I'd better get on home. It's too cold to stand out here talking," Skip said.

"Good night," Bo Jack said and went inside.

Three days later, a knock sounded on the front door after lunch.

"Let me see who it is," Bo Jack said and went through the living area to the less-used front door.

He opened it and found a smiling man a few years older than him standing there. The man's bright blue eyes twinkled. "Are you Bo Jack?"

"Yes, sir, I am."

"I'm Harley. Did your mother tell you I'd be stopping by?"

Bo Jack took an instant liking to the man. "Come on in, sir."

"Just call me Harley. When did you get home?"

"Tuesday morning—you're timing's lucky. I'd hoped to find a way to see my aunt today, but you got here first."

Mama appeared in the doorway leading to the kitchen. "Hello, Harley. Take off your coat. It's good to see you again. Would you like some coffee?"

"It's nice to see you. Yes, ma'am. Thank you."

Mama disappeared and Bo Jack motioned to the chairs by the window.

"Please, sit down."

Harley shrugged out of his jacket and placed it on the arm of the chair before he sank down onto the upholstered seat.

Mama returned with a cup and handed it to their guest. "Here you go."

Harley took it and smiled. "Thank you, ma'am."

"You boys have a good visit. I need to walk to the store. I'll be back after a while. You two take your time." Mama returned to the kitchen, and in a few minutes, the door opened and closed.

Harley blew a cooling breath over the rim of his steaming cup and took a sip of coffee.

"Mama says you need another man for your crew," Bo Jack said.

Harley set his cup and saucer on the small table beside him. He nodded. "Yes, sir, we do. It's not easy work. Have you ever taken down a tree or climbed one to remove some limbs?"

"No, sir, but I've climbed a few just for fun."

Harley laughed but fixed him with his piercing gaze. "I hear you know how to work. You've got a lot to learn. You can't fool around—someone might get hurt and it could be you in this business. We have several contracts in Texas this next year. The one we're working right now is in a town called Longview, Texas."

"Never heard of it."

"It's in the eastern portion of the state. Once it ends, we have other ones coming up in Jasper, Silsbee, and Port Arthur. Even more are possible. We get the job done right and on time. Two of my cousins work with me. I'll train you, if you're willing to learn."

This felt right. Bo Jack stood up and stuck out his hand. "I accept, sir. When do we leave?"

Harley stood and shook it. "Sunday morning. I'll come by and pick you up at seven."

"I'll be ready."

Bo Jack walked him to the door. He returned to his room and stared at his suitcase. Good thing he hadn't unpacked much. From what Harley had said, he'd better get used to staying packed and ready to go.

****

He had no idea what an understatement his thought had been. Once they arrived in Texas, the whirlwind of work never stopped. They finished in Longview and went to Jasper for contracts. They finished there and needed a couple of more men for the next contract job, so when he heard from Lowell and found out he needed a job, he called him.

Lowell and another friend from home joined them in Silsbee for tree contracts. From there, they went to Port Arthur and then returned to Jasper for another job. At this point, one of Harley's cousins transferred, Lowell returned home, and their other friend from home headed to another crew. Bo Jack liked the job and working for Harley.

Harley picked him up for work one morning with news. "I got a call last night about you. The state supervisor wants to know if I think you're ready to handle a crew on your own."

"Why? Are you leaving?"

"No. He wants you to transfer to Houston where your other friend just transferred. You'd be his boss."

"What did you tell the supervisor?"

"I said you're as ready as you'll ever be. You've done a good job and learned fast. They might even want to send you to arboriculture school."

184

"What?"

Harley laughed. "One thing at a time. I sure hate to lose you, but you should take this. I'll let you get a taste of it here before you transfer."

Bo Jack arrived in Houston on Halloween night in 1956. Having a friend from home on the crew made taking it over easier. In February 1957, they sent him to Arboriculture school in Kent, Ohio. Once he finished, he returned to Houston.

His love of history made his next assignment exciting. They went to Shanghai Pierce's ranch close to Wharton, Texas, to work on the trees there. Then they went to San Antonio for a couple of contracts, including one at the Alamo to work on the trees there.

After jobs like those, returning to Houston and driving out to Alvin every day to take moss out of live oak trees didn't compare. By this time, some company issues concerned him and he quit and went to work for another tree company, but his former boss called him and convinced him to come back to them.

Staying at a rooming house worked best for his nomadic schedule. One night in November 1957, Bo Jack came in from a job and couldn't find anyone home at the rooming house. Where could everyone be? He changed clothes and freshened up a bit. The rooming house remained deserted, so he decided to go down to the Jersey Bell for some games and a beer.

A tall redheaded man stood in front of the baseball pinball machine.

"Hey, Irish," Bo Jack said. "Where is everyone tonight?"

"I don't know. You're the first friend I've seen tonight. You want to try a game on this machine with me?"

"Sure."

Bo Jack stepped in front of Irish and handed him his bottle. He positioned his hands on either side of the machine. Irish pushed the button and Bo Jack focused on the lift of the metal flap releasing the ball, using the levers to spring the ball across the baseball diamond and into the slot crevice. The toy baseball players moved around the bases in the glass box at the top. The ding, ding, ding sounded a home run.

"All right," Bo Jack said.

"You lucky stiff."

Bo Jack laughed and moved to the side of the machine. Irish handed him his beer and pushed the game button. He tilted the machine a bit as the metal ball rolled forward.

"That's not going to help. You—" Something red caught Bo Jack's eye. He stopped watching the game. A red dress distracted him. The woman wearing the red dress suspended any rational thought from his head. Her long auburn hair caught the light. He forgot to breathe.

A man escorted the woman to a small table.

"Hey, Bo Jack. It's your turn," Irish said.

Bo Jack exhaled and used a slang term.

The waitress set a beer in front of the man and a small coke in front of the woman.

The man glanced up at Bo Jack. "Hey, you."

Irish turned. "Are you talking to me?"

Bo Jack elbowed him. "No, he's talking to me."

"Were you in Korea?"

"No, but a work buddy of mine was. He uses that slang word. Guess I've picked it up."

"Oh, okay. You want to join us?"

"Sure."

Irish shrugged and returned to the game.

Bo Jack took a deep breath, a drink of his beer, and headed to the table.

The man extended his hand. "I'm Ted."

"I'm Bo Jack," he said, shaking the man's hand. Bo Jack pulled out a chair and took a seat. His breath caught when the bluest pair of eyes he'd ever seen met his. She smiled and his heart missed a beat.

"This is Bonnie."

"It's nice to meet you, Bo Jack," she said.

"We missed our bus to go downtown to a movie we wanted to see, so we stopped in here," Ted said.

Bonnie took a sip from her small bottle of coke. She didn't fit in a place like this.

"I don't have a car, so we're going to have to wait on the next bus," Ted said.

"I have a car," Bo Jack said. "I can take you downtown or anywhere you need."

"That's nice of you, but we've missed the show. We'll just finish our drinks and the next bus will be here to go home."

"Suit yourselves. The offer stands if you change your mind."

Bonnie crossed her legs—shapely calves curved to slender ankles and feet. The black patent leather heels she wore accentuated her assets.

Bo Jack turned his head and Irish caught his eye and winked.

"What do you do, Bo Jack?" Bonnie asked.

He turned back and almost lost his breath again. Those baby blue eyes—

"I am a crew boss for one of the tree companies," he said.

"That can be dangerous work," Ted said.

Bo Jack shrugged. "I like it. It's an adventure every day." More people came in and Bo Jack scanned the room. "Hey, this place is about full. Do you two want to go for some coffee at the Prince Drive-In?"

Bonnie smiled at Ted. "I'd like that."

"Okay, then, but what about the bus?"

"I don't mind if he drives us home," Bonnie said.

"Fine by me. Let's go then." Ted paid the ticket, and they headed to Bo Jack's car. Once they reached the drive-in, Ted excused himself to go to the restroom.

"Do you have a pen?" Bonnie asked.

"Sure," Bo Jack reached in his shirt pocket and handed it to her.

She opened her purse and took out a piece of paper. "Why don't I give you my phone number and we can double date sometime?"

He watched her face for clues to see if she meant more, but no, she gave him a sweet smile.

She must like Ted. Still— "That sounds fine," he said.

"Good." She wrote her number on the small piece of paper and handed it to him.

The carhop came to the window. "What will it be? You can't just park here."

"Three coffees."

Ted returned, and they chatted for about another hour. Bo Jack found out she had worked for the phone company while going to college classes and now worked for a loan company. She came from a small town and had left home the day after she graduated from high school.

Bonnie grew silent when he asked more questions, and Ted piped in with questions for Bo Jack.

The drive-in closed, and they took Bonnie to her apartment building first. Bo Jack waited in the car while Ted walked her to the door. After a few minutes, Ted returned to the car. He slid inside and shut the door.

"Ready to go?" Bo Jack asked.

Ted shifted in his seat to face him.

"Bonnie said she gave you her number so we can double date sometime. That sounds fine, but there's something you should know. Bonnie and I are just friends. We are good friends. She was engaged, but her fiancé's plane crashed, and everyone on board died. It's been a hard year for her."

Something protective stirred inside Bo Jack. He hurt for her heartbreak. All the other things he'd been feeling about her faded in significance. "That's rough. No one should go through that, but we're not in control."

Ted nodded. "You're right about that."

Bo Jack dropped Ted at his place and headed to the rooming house. He couldn't sleep for thinking about Bonnie.

By the time he got up the next day, he knew he'd be smarter not to call her. He fought thoughts of her all day, but by that night, he lost the battle. He swallowed hard, picked up the receiver, hesitated, and settled it back in the cradle. After two more attempts, his finger dialed her number. "Hello. May I please speak to Bonnie?"

"This is she."

"Hello, Bonnie. This is Bo Jack."

"Hello. How are you?"

"Fine. Listen, I know you gave me your number to go on a double date, but I'd like to take you out sometime. Ted tells me you two are just friends."

Silence.

"Bonnie, are you still there?"

"Yes, I'm here. I don't know if that is a good idea. Maybe Ted and I can just go to the drive-in with you again sometime—as friends."

Disappointment silenced him.

"Bo Jack?"

"Thank you for your honesty, but I need to be honest too, Bonnie. I'm more interested in you than that."

"I'm sorry. I like you, but I don't want to go out alone with you. Can't we just be friends?"

"I don't know."

"Think about it. Good-bye."

Bo Jack did think about it, but she had his heart in a mess. So he called her again. She turned him down again and again and again.

For the next couple of weeks, Bo Jack worked and thought of little else besides Bonnie. He called her again on Friday. "May I speak to Bonnie?"

"This is she. Bo Jack?"

"Yeah, I'm not giving up."

Silence.

"Will you go to church with me, Bo Jack?"

What? His heart slowed. "What?"

"Will you go to church with me on Sunday?"

His heart jumped. He didn't hesitate. "Yes, I'd be happy to go to church with you."

"Good. You can pick me up at ten o'clock."

Bo Jack wished he could see her face, although he could hear a smile in her voice. "I'll be there. Good-bye." He held the back of the phone receiver to his mouth and smiled before hanging it up and saying a prayer. He thought about his life. What adventures he'd had. None of them compared to Bonnie. The home he wanted shone in her eyes. She could be the biggest adventure of all.

About the Author

Lana Lynne Higginbotham (writes in the fiction genre under the pen name: *Lana* Lynne): Lana is a Speech-Language Pathologist and a writer/author. She is the author of these historical fiction novels under her pen name, Lana Lynne: *Home Always Beckons: A New Sunrise (*First Publication 2009; Second Edition 2018*); Trails of Change: A New Sunset* (First Publication 2010; Second Edition 2018); *Sunbeams at Twilight: A Life's Echo (First* Publication 2012-first printing 2012, second printing 2014, Second Edition 2018) and *A Compass of Stars in Her Eyes (*First Publication 2018*)*.

Her first contemporary Christian Fiction novella is *Whimsy Michaels and Her Amazing Room (*First publication 2018).

The Adventures of Bo Jack (2019) is her first historical fiction novella based on/inspired by a family member's childhood memories.

Other writing credits: A creative nonfiction novel, written with a coauthor: *Life Between the Letters: The Chuck and Mary Felder Story (*First Publication 2014*)* by Lana Lynne Higginbotham and Mary K. Felder. Blog writer: a weekly blog post (2012-2014) contributor and served as part of the "Venture Galleries Author Collection" blog team (2013) under her pen name, Lana Lynne.

Lana lives with her husband in East Texas. They are empty nesters and proud grandparents. Learn more by visiting www.lanalynne.com (Links to my Twitter, Facebook, Instagram, Pinterest, and Amazon can be found there).

Please leave a review on Amazon and take time to like my Facebook author page: Lana Lynne.